Conniption Fit

Copyright © 2020 by Rene Cheri

Any references to historical events, real people, or real places are used fictitiously. Names, characters, and places are products of the author's imagination.

ISBN: 9798563976511

Published by: Nakeisha Unlimited, LLC

Table of Contents

Release

Jericha stood tall and beautiful in the middle of the nightclub. Her clothing bold as she was here to make a statement. For someone that did not know her she looked the part. She walked in as if she owned the place. Shoulders straight, head held high. The fire in her eyes matching her mood. She had to cloak herself in anger to remove any remnants of fear or nervousness. Her heart skittered and skipped and for a second, she questioned why she was even there. She people watched for a while, holding a glass of some fruity concoction that made her head spin slightly after the first sip. The drinks were always strong, encouraging a looseness of virtue and pockets. She was not sure if it was the drink or the anticipation of what was to come that had her feeling off and a little lightheaded. Afterall she had only taken a sip, as she sought the normal effects of calming her nerves.

She placed the glass on the bar and glanced around as everyone danced closely. The bass of the music seemed to sync with the beat of her heart. There was just a hint of uncertainty, but it was drowned out by the dull ache that could be felt deep within her soul. She was tired. She was tired of running and hiding.

Goosebumps tingled across her skin as nerve impulses scattered in every direction. Bodies were touching, swaying as they seemed to absorb energy from each touch, embrace, and breath. This was the only connection here. Sexual, sensual, and raw need. There was no need for conversation. It was communicated in the way they moved, backs arched, breast to chest, backsides to torso. Even the smoked swirled in the air creating a more seductive environment.

She shivered as she felt like she was on display for everyone to see. As if everyone could feel her discomfort and knew that she no longer belonged. She watched one couple as the man took the lead. She recalled a time when she was caught up in this world of seduction, money, and sex. It was another world separated from everything and everyone else. Their dance told a story. She watched remembering her own story. Her cheek tingled as if just the mere thought sent a reminder to its receptors of the stinging pain felt from his slap across her face.

Again, she'd done nothing to provoke his anger. Just a smile could send him into a tyrant, leaving her at the receiving end of what he deemed her punishment to be. For a second, anger had replaced the fear and humiliation that kept her from fighting back. Hanging on to this, it simmered and then exploded. She'd finally had enough. She felt as if it was burning a hole in her gut and fueled a pent-up rage that had been building for years. She stood still and rigid as her mind took her back. Though for anyone watching, they'd think she was entranced by the dance that unfolded before her.

A vase crashed into the wall, mere inches from his head. She wasn't sure if he was speaking or if it was all in her mind because it had been drilled into her very existence repeatedly. She was worthless, a whore, unattractive, useless, and good for nothing. He'd said so many times that he loved her so much, but in the same breath grab her by the throat yelling "but it isn't enough for this bitch!" He looked up in shock. Through the fog of drunkenness, she noted a glint of confusion and surprise in his eyes. It was the first time she'd ever respond other than cowering in fear or rushing to reassure him that she could be everything that he wanted her to be. She was too afraid to even raise her voice at him. But that night, the rage screamed in her ears to fight. "I am so sick of being a good woman to your sorry ass!" Her mother would have shuttered and turned over in her grave had she heard the words that came from her mouth.

"Fuck your rollercoaster of I'm sorry(s) and I love you(s)!" Anything within reach shot across the room, jet fueled by a woman who had finally reached her breaking point. He stood watching her, and as if in slow motion, she saw the change in his eyes. The surprise was replaced with a cold hard stare.

"You bitch!" he yelled. "Who the hell do you think you are? I promise you are going to regret that." He took a step towards her and she bolted from the room. He chased her down the hall, grabbing her by her hair and slamming her against the wall. "You must have a death wish" he growled in her ear. Pushing her up against the wall. "Since you want to act like a little bitch, let me show you what little bitches get." He shoved his knee between her legs and ripped her pants and underwear down. His sick ass was turned on by it all. He slapped her butt before shoving his fingers up in her. He pressed himself up against her and she could feel him hardened against her.

It wouldn't be the first time he raped her in anger. But that night she couldn't take it. She'd rather die. She hadn't realized she'd said it out loud. He seemed to enjoy it all. She shoved her elbow into his gut with all her strength and ran to the room. She ran for the closet grabbing the revolver that rested on the top shelf. He used it as a constant reminder to her that he could end her life at any time. It was always loaded. He preferred it that way. He'd groomed her early on.

Fear and manipulation alone could make someone forget all common sense and behave in any manner that their aggressor wants. She'd never touched it. It never occurred to her to use it against him. She hated guns. She hated the sound, the feel of the cold metal. It was a cold representation of death. She'd seen what it could do to another person. But it was time she used his own words against him. She repeated it verbatim as they were etched in her mind. She'd become accustomed to hearing him say it daily. Except a resounding smack, push or punch would follow his words.

She didn't recognize her own voice as she whispered with a raised brow. "Do you know that I could kill you? No one would ever know or even care." She felt as if someone else had taken control of her body. She removed the safety. Though she hated guns, she knew her way around one. She pointed at his head and pulled the trigger. It exploded into the wall inches above his head. He stopped suddenly and raised his hands. "Ok Jerri, ok you got me. Come on, give me the gun." She walked to him slowly. She raised the gun to his head pushing the barrel into his forehead. Her hand was steady. Her voice strong. "Jail clothing does nothing for this figure I've tried to hide just to satisfy you. Otherwise, that bullet up there would have been right here in your forehead. You got that *bitch*?" You can have all of this" he waved her hand. "I am done, and you are not going to follow me or try to find me or make any contact with me ever. Do you hear me!" she yelled. "After tonight, forget you ever knew me or the next time I won't miss. Or maybe I'll just poison your ass, kill you in your sleep, better yet paralyze you. Watch you suffer…you get my drift?"

She walked backwards from the room. The gun still pointed at him. She took one last glance around her dream home. It was stunning, everything a girl could ask for. But behind closed doors, it turned into a nightmare. It was all that she had. He was all that she had. But she'd rather have nothing if having anything was what she lived for the last few years. On her 18th birthday, she lost everything. He'd taken her innocence, her joy; he'd taken her life. She still couldn't believe she'd given anyone that power over her. No house, money, lifestyle or man woman was worth that.

The anger was still burning in her chest when she jumped in the car. But beneath it all for the first time in a long time she felt relief. She was free. In that moment she knew that she could never go back. The very life that she just fought for would surely be ended if she did. She also knew that she would never make it through another night or day in that hell hole, she'd probably end it herself if she had to.

She cranked the engine, put the car in gear and drove off. She hadn't made it a mile before she pulled over, opened the door, and emptied the contents of her stomach onto the ground. She held her breath as car lights approached her from behind. But they slowed then drove around her. She had left with only the clothes on her back. Thankfully, her purse was still in the car after she returned from grocery shopping. She was only a few minutes late from her allotted time and that was all it took to send her day into a downward spiral.

The beginning-----

Jericha left home at the age of 16. She lived the next few years mostly on the streets. She developed early and was curvy and cute. At the age of 12, she'd realized that she attracted older men. Even her father watched her in a way that no father or man should watch a child. She'd caught him a few times, eyes lingering or hanging around in her bedroom door. He seemed to have timed her whenever she showered because he'd be in the hall. She started to expect him to be there so she would dart from the bathroom to her room in a towel. Soon after she'd always make sure to carry her clothing in the bathroom with her and dress before coming out. She didn't understand at the time, why it made her un-comfortable, but it was something about the way he watched her that made her stomach turn.

Her mother must have felt the same way because she'd never leave her alone with him. It was around that time that her mother started asking her questions about her body and if anyone had ever tried to touch her in places that they shouldn't. Her mother explained to her about men and woman and men and little girls. How it was ok for a man to be with a woman like that, but no man should be with a child, and she was still a child until she told her she wasn't. She'd taught her about being aware of her surroundings to include being mindful of the clothing she wore. She didn't want to advertise any-thing that she didn't have available to sell or give away. She'd warned her that people would try to take advantage of her and not to trust any man. Even family members. They were sometimes the worst ones. She'd told her that she could come to her about anything and that in their home, they did not hold any secrets. But those doing wrong loved to have secrets.

Her father was 10 years older than her mother. She learned later that her parents started messing around when her mother was only 13 and he was 23. He'd told her that she was mature enough to be his woman, but that she had to keep it a secret because her parents would not allow them to be together. They snuck around until she was 16 and mother got pregnant. Her parents forced her to have an abortion and they threatened to go to the police if he'd ever contacted her again. But the damage had already been done. Her mother thought that sex had made her grown and she wanted to live by her own rules. She had her first taste and she wanted more. She ran away from home to be with different boys and men. Her preference was men. Jericha's father moved away, but once her mother turned 18, he came back for her as he'd promised. She was already pregnant with Jericha when she moved in with him. Though her father had wondering eyes. He never touched her or even said anything inappropriate to her. She believed he knew just how crazy her mother was. Her wrath would be far worse than anything her own father or uncles could ever do when it came to her baby girl. She would have killed him and happily went to jail for it.

After Jericha was born, her mother started going to church. She made sure to keep Jericha in the church. But the more she praised God, the more her husband strayed. The whole concept of church meant well, but it was people that tarnished what should have been a sanctuary. The men in the church were worse than the men she encountered in the streets.

She remembered at the age of 14 or 15, one of the deacons pushing her up against the wall and whispering to her, "I can't help myself. I've waited so long to just touch your beautiful skin. Has anyone ever told you how beautiful you are?" She could smell the stench of alcohol on his breath. His ragged beard was rough against her neck as he inhaled her scent. "Mmm, I just want to smell it" he whispered as he ran his thick hands up her skirt. "See, I knew you were primed and ready. I can take real good care of you. Anything you want." She waited, calculating the right time. She smiled and that was enough for him to let down his guard. He was excited at the prospect of her letting him touch her. That was when she lifted her knee as hard as she could into his groin. He swallowed a grunt and doubled over wheezing. "You stupid little…"

"You sick pervert! My mom warned me about you nasty old men!" She kicked him in the behind as hard as she could and ran from the room right into her mother in the hall. Her mom looked at her disheveled clothing and glared towards the door. "Who you letting feel you up girl? Whose son head I gotta go up aside?"

She stuttered "Ma, no. It was deacon…" but her mom cut her off before finishing. "Go on up to Mrs. Denise's room and wait for me. Jericha took off running and her mother whispered loudly after her "Slow down, fix your clothing and don't go running your mouth to anyone. Momma always told you that you didn't have to be afraid of anyone. I got you." With that, she turned towards the door and marched up into that room. Instead of doing as she was told, she tip-toed quietly up to the door. She leaned against it, straining to hear what she could. Their voices were muffled. But she mostly heard her mom's voice. It wasn't long after she heard footsteps. The door swung open, and he shuffled his way out of the room and down the hall. He had a slight limp as he hurriedly went out of the building. Her mother came out after him. A scowl on her face as she wiped off the tip of her pocketknife with his handkerchief and dropped it into the wide pockets of her dark, wide skirt. She'd never seen that deacon again at church after that mor-ning.

For some reason she attracted every want-to-be sugar daddy and low-key pedophile on the block. Many begged to touch her or taste her. Licking their crusty lips and scratching their scruffy beards. Others would hide behind a hug or pat as they secretly glided their filthy hands against her skin or groped her. She always managed to get around the lingering hands or brooding looks. Never staying anywhere long and always making sure she traveled in a group, never alone.

Though she lived in a far from perfect household, her mother taught her about Jesus, and the difference between having religion and having a personal relation-ship with God. She'd taught her how to pray. Though she swore God never heard her prayers. Her mother shared with her the many hardships she faced herself while growing up. How her uncles and male cousins taught her about sex way before she should have known what it was.

She taught her about the streets, drugs, street walkers, prostitutes and the many "corporate" men and husbands who sought them out late at night in alleys, corners, and backseats. She warned her that the world wanted nothing more than to see her fail. But God wanted her to soar above it all and show everyone that she was queen. Her mother always reminded her that she was capable of anything she set her mind to.

She didn't need to depend on a man or anyone else but herself. But her world as she knew it, ended one rainy evening during her senior year in high school. It would change the course of her life forever. She was an honor roll student and she received multiple offers to colleges. She'd dreamed of going to an HBSCU school. She fell in love watching the college students. The idea of going to college, living on campus, and perhaps pledging to one of the sororities all captivated her. She loved to read about successful black women and men.

Many came through the trenches, and surprisingly belonged to a sorority or fraternity. She was in her room reading one evening. The rain quietly beating against her window. The wind was picking up and seemed to moan as it crept through the trees and cracks of her building. Her father rushed up to her rooming yelling her name. She could hear the panic in his voice. "Jerri, we gotta go. Something has happened. It's your mom sweetie. She's been in an accident."

She sat up, dropping her book onto her bed. The pages flipping erratically before settling. Echoing her thoughts and heart. "Is she ok?" Panic already setting in. "I don't know. We have to hurry. She was rushed to the hospital. One of the nurses said it doesn't look good."

They learned that her mother had been struck by a vehicle as she crossed the street. The driver hadn't seen her as they frantically rushed their own child to the emergency room. They rushed to the hospital, but it was too late. She sat in the cold, small, private room in the emergency room. She held her father's hand as doctor told them they had done all they could do for her mother. She was strong, but she had too many injuries and didn't survive the accident. Neither of them cried. They were told to take as much time as they needed, as a nurse rambled on and handed her father pamphlets and contact info. They asked if there was anyone else that they wanted them to contact, but there was no one else.

Her grandparents passed away a year apart, 2 years ago. It was just the two of them left. Her father left her with the nurse when they took him back to see her. The nurse held her hand and prayed with her and over her. She told her that she knew her mom. That she was one of the strongest and brightest women that she knew. She told her that her mother spoke of her often and she loved her more than anything and was so proud of her. She even gave her her number and told her to call anytime if she needed anything.

Her father returned and she knew something had broken within him. Her mother took a part of him with her. They rode home in silence. The once calming sound of rain now filled her head loudly. She could hear every drop as she watched them crash onto the window. Her father didn't know what to say to her. He couldn't even look her in the eyes.

She sat for hours on her bed. She kept her blinds opened as she watched the driveway waiting for her mother to pull up as she did every evening. She prayed to God fervently that it wasn't true. That her mother would walk through the door and say it was someone else that was hit that night. But she never came. She couldn't keep up with her thoughts as she tried to remember every thought of her mother, pictured her smile, her round face with her curly hair and bold eyes.

Finally, something broke inside of her and she screamed out when she realized that her mother wasn't coming back. Her father ran up the stairs, but he seemed afraid to step pass the doorway. She threw things around her room, tearing pages from her books and kicking things over. A photo of her mother fell from the shelf. It was of her mother embracing her from behind, it landed face up. She stopped abruptly and fell to her knees touching her mother's face.

She was such a beautiful woman. They had the same eyes as they stared back at her frozen in time. She kissed the photo as she cried, begging her mother to come home. Her father eventually came into her room. He stood behind her, tears falling down his face. He kneeled on the floor and gathered her in his arms and held her. He held her there for God knows how long. They both cried uncontrollably.

But, during a time when he should have been comforting her his hands began to wander, first gently rubbing her shoulders, then her back before brushing against her behind. She didn't realize what was happening until it was too late, and he began cupping her behind and rubbing her roughly. He'd turned his head into her neck, and she realized that it wasn't his wet tears that she felt against her skin, but his lips and tongue. She froze and a chill ran up her spine. But he seemed to not realize it as he continued exploring her body. She tried to speak but he kissed her. "Shhhh baby, let me make you feel better." He was whispering to her about how beautiful she was just like her mother and how he was going to miss her. He began speaking of her mother, but then he started saying how he'd watched her for years. How he always wanted to touch her.

"Let daddy take care of you." It was as if he struck her. She shoved him away, he stood glaring at her as her chest rose and fell and she gulped for her breath.

He watched her chest as he ran his hands through his hair. "I'm sorry, he stammered. For a second, I thought you were your mother. I...I...I... wanted you to be." He looked up into her eyes reaching out and touching her hair. "You look so much like her. I could, we could make each other feel better. Just for tonight." He must have seen the disgust in her eyes because he faltered. "Wait, it's not like that. You must know by now that I am not your real father. I could never feel this way about my own child. There would be nothing wrong about it. You're a woman now and I am a man. I've seen the way you've watched me. Prancing around showing off your body."

He took her hand and guided it to his lap. Cupping her hand into his he tried to rub her against his erection, but she snatched her hand away. She slapped him and ran to the restroom. She quickly locked the door behind her and began vomiting into the toilet. She vomited until she had nothing else to bring up. Exhausted, she hugged the cold porcelain and cried until she was drained and spent. He came to the door several times throughout the night. Apologizing, saying that he didn't know what had come over him. He just didn't know how to cope with the loss. He tried telling her it was the only way he knew how to comfort her. She slept on the floor the of the bathroom that night.

During the early hours of the morning, she crept out of the restroom. She picked up the photo of her and her mother together, smiling, and happy. She packed a small bag of clothing and grabbed her school bag easing the front door open, trying to be as quiet as she could in the still home. That morning started a new journey in her life. A life without her mother, or father. Her mother was dead and after last night so was her father as far as she was concerned.

She bounced between friends' homes for the first year. Explaining to questioning parents that her father was having a hard time coping with the loss of her mother and she was home alone most of the time anyway. Though they tried to reach out to her, she only felt empty and lost. She left one home after another, whenever she felt she wore out her welcome or when too many questions were being asked.

She would go home from time to time and walk the empty rooms reminiscing about her mother. Her father was hardly ever there, and she made sure to go there when he was gone. She was sure he knew that she was coming by because he kept the refrigerator stocked. She thought he must have seen her closet become scarcer and scarcer. But she never laid eyes on him again after that night.

She ran the streets for about a year. Rebelling, drinking and even dabbling in drugs. Mostly marijuana, but somehow, she managed to make it to school every morning and pass her classes maintaining her GPA. She frequented night clubs and bars because the noise was a distraction from falling into the pits of depression that kept creeping up in her head. There were unwanted thoughts, along with the panic of anxiety that she kept at bay almost daily.

She met Jarohn in one of those bars. He'd always watch her from a distance but never approached her.

One night her and her friends stumbled past him, and he'd reached out grabbing her arm preventing her from falling flat on her face. He was really good looking. But what drew her to him more so was his calm demeaner. He was always so serious looking and carried a level of confidence that she herself wished that she had. It reminded her of her mother, she carried that same level of confidence. After steadying her he looked into her eyes, something else he always did "Aren't you a bit young to be out so late beautiful. Isn't past your bedtime? What's your name anyway?" She couldn't muster one of her usual smart responses and she stared up at him. There was a hint of a smile just beyond his stare. He was still holding her hand as he slowly perused her body from head to toe. Her cheeks warmed as she apologized. There was something about the way that he stared at her that made her wish she were that confident woman. Her friends were behind her giggling and she heard one of them say "damn he's fine." They egged her on, so she reached up and ran her fingers in his hair. "So are you going to tell me your name," he asked again? Her knees trembled.

"Jericha." "Well, Jericha" spinning her around. "You should come and dance with me" he pulled her close and her friends were cheering her on! She wrapped her arms around his neck and stood on her tippy toes as she swayed her hips in rhythm with his. She put on her best effort to sound seductive.

"Bedtime? Sure, it could be my bedtime. Are you coming to tuck me in daddy?" She leaned back looking into his eyes. He laughed out loud drawing her eyes to his mouth. She ran her thumb across his bottom lip and he quickly still her hand in his. She recognized the hunger in his eyes, but he didn't let her go any further. "I sure can one-night baby girl. But not tonight. Your friends are waiting for you" he nodded his head in their direction. She walked off shaking her head and hips "Your loss." As she turned the corner she glanced back, he was leaning on the bar watching her. His smiled spread when he saw her turn. She faintly registered her girls' voices in the background "damn girl you know you can't handle him. That is all man right there." After that night she had become a regular to the bar in hopes of running into him. He was sometimes there but he hadn't approached her again. She'd catch his hooded eyes on her many times though. She enjoyed the bar scene. There was really no security, and anyone could get in if you looked the part. Especially the ladies. The liquor flowed and so did the drugs. A guy had offered her a line of coke once asking if she'd ever tried it. She hadn't but was thinking what the hell. But before she had a chance to wonder off with him Jarohn was behind her. He had a way of showing up out of know where to her rescue. He pulled her behind him. "Looks like your about to get yourself into some trouble you won't be able to get out of young lady." He gave the guy a deadly look and he decided to move on. "I don't want to ever see you using any of that shit there. He raised her chin making her meet his eyes. You're too gorgeous to be a junky" leaving her shaken and feeling like a child being crushed for her behavior. He started talking with her after that night. With each encounter she would indulge him with a little more about herself. He started giving her cash and told her to come to him if she ever needed anything. He took on a big brother/protector role, though she tried hard to get him to see her as more. He'd always ask her how was school going and if she was being a good girl. He'd seem to know when she'd had her limit of drinks and would give the bartender a slight wave and she'd be cut off for the night. She'd hang around late hoping to see when he would leave but he seemed to never go home.

On her 18th birthday she looked for Jarohn at the bar. She made sure she'd carefully dressed in a black liquid jumper that fit her so closely one would think it was painted on her. The sleeves and sides were held with thin netting leaving her smooth skin on display from shoulder to ankle. She knew the effect she had on men by now and had had her fair share of sexual encounters. But she'd never had who she really wanted, which was Jarohn. She wore a tiara on her head and heels that drew attention to her powerful calves and derriere with every step. Every man appreciated her when she walked whistling and yelling out cat calls, but she was on a mission. She'd decided that she would have him at all costs and now she was officially a woman. He actually found her before she found him. He approached her from behind whispering in her ear "is it someone's birthday today?" She turned and as usual her heart skipped before revving up. Her body purred in his presence.

"It sure is and guess who's 18 tonight?" she responded. "Let me guess" he said with a smile. She knew that he liked what she wore for him. He circled her slowly as a cat did when it toyed with a its meal before devouring it. He placed his arm around her shoulders asking if she was ready to go with him tonight and she was more than ready. He signaled a guy that appeared out of nowhere. He moved to his side quickly. "Sir?" "Jericha here is ready to go."

He approached her and told her to come with him. She turned to Jarohn with clear confusion on her face. He smiled "Oh? Perhaps you've forgotten about the invitation you'd given me to tuck you in?" She smiled back liking where this was leading. "Well then, no questions just do as I say. Go with him." She swallowed, not sure what she was getting herself in, but she followed. No questions asked. The guy whom she had nicknamed Blue in her mind because, well, he looked like he could be named Blue. He led and she followed through doors that she had never realized were there. It led down a dark hall, but she continued to feel the pulsations of the base through the walls. They went through another set of doors and were out on a back entrance where a dark sedan was waiting. He motioned towards the car. "She'll take you to your next stop." She wasn't afraid because others were outside as well. There were less people than the crowded front entrance but, they were there, nonetheless. Some were hanging out hanging out talking while some women were leaning into car windows or stepping into similar vehicles. The window had lowered, and Blue stepped back. She walked cautiously to the car. She wasn't a complete fool in love. She was relieved when she saw a woman in the driver's seat. She had curly red hair and oddly piercing grey eyes which clashed with her dark skin. She wondered if she had colored contacts. "Come on around and get in the front seat," she said. Her voice just as intoxicating as her face. "My name is Grayce." She caught a slight accent, realizing that she wasn't American. The door unlocked and she got in. The girl chatted with her about really nothing. She asked her age and Jericha told her that she was out celebrating her 18th birthday. Which she received a nod in response. She hummed along with the bouncy music playing in the background. "Relax, it's really a privilege and an experience that you'll enjoy." With that Jericha sat back in the seat and listened to the music. They arrived at another upscaled club. The clubs she frequented on the other side of town paled in comparison. Grayce turned to her saying "Get ready girl, and welcome to Creed." Jericha jumped out and Grayce sped off before she had a chance to close the door completely. The glass doors opened, and a guy came out holding his hand out for her. She placed hers into his and he smiled in appreciation. She thought to herself that a girl could get use to all of this, the men associated with Jarohn all seemed to be good looking. The place was stunning. Everything and everyone screamed money. It was a nightclub on steroids. As she looked around, she realized it was more than just a club. It reminded her of a fancy hotel with several nightclubs and bars within it. He led her to an elevator and handed her a keycard. Room 225 and Mr. Creed will be in touch. Even the elevator was luxurious. The walls were glass and she looked down really impressed, beautiful lights danced below. The elevator stopped on what she assumed was her floor. She walked down the hall and found room 225. The room was more like a mini apartment. It was equipped with a kitchen, bathroom, and king-sized bed. The door clicked shut behind her not thinking she reached for the handle to look back out into the hall. But, to her surprise the door was locked from the outside. She had goosebumps run across her arm and she thought back to one of her mother's favorite sayings, she could almost hear her voice "Girl everything that glitters ain't gold and fool's gold cost you much more!" She rubbed her arms and walked around the room. She found a note on the bed. It was printed on a gold and black card. *Hey beautiful. Don't worry. I promise you that you will not regret this.* She'd only seen rooms like this on tv and in magazines. She went into the bathroom and stared at her reflection in the mirror. She was touching up her makeup when she heard the door open. She looked behind her in the mirror. Her hand in midair until Jarohn's reflection behind her. She smiled thinking finally. She turned and walked towards him.

"How do you like the place" he asked? "Are you kidding me?" "Creeds my baby. It is all mines." She was really impressed as she listened to him go on about how he had brought his dreams to life. She was listening to him, but her eyes were focused on his mouth. She watched as his words formed across his lips.

He cleared his throat. "Are you listening to me?" "Yes" and repeated what he'd just said. "So, the question is, why am I here?" "Well let's just say that you are about to receive the best lullaby and bed tucking a girl could ask for." "So, when do we start?" she asked seductively.

"Come to me" he commanded. She walked up to him slowly. Trying her best at seduction. That's what they always did in those love stories she watched. When she stood before him, he reached out and gripped her neck. Not threatening, but he had enough pressure to make her gasp. He leaned down and kissed her. She melted in his arms. She was sure that she was in a puddle at his feet. But he stopped as suddenly as he started. "Not yet, beautiful. We have all night. Let me show you the club." She followed him impressed with his self-control. Most guys would be all over her by now. She knew that he wanted her. She saw it in his eyes as he pulled away from her. He laced his fingers through hers and they walked down the hall together. The club had several layers. Each level drastically different from the other however it all fit. There was a stark contrast in the music, the people and how they dressed. Everyone knew him and rushed over, either getting out of his way or to assist him. He waved them off and gave her a personal tour of his place. Some areas were playful and light, while others were soulful leaving a feeling of longing. The lower that

they went the more captivating the place became.
Everything about the last level was dark. The music, the
feeling. Windows were everywhere. She not only heard
music. Behind the glass were sounds of passion. Both
men and woman. There was laughter, moans and from
some screams.

"So Jericha. Do you think you are ready for a
man like me?" he asked. "I'm nothing like most guys."
She nodded her head. His eyes darkened. He lifted her
chin. "First off we use words here. Say it." She
swallowed "yes". She was growing tired of the suspense.
Come on let's get it on already she said in her head.
"Turn around" he demanded. She did, wondering why
did he have her facing a dark window "Touch it."
"Touch what?" He came up close behind her. He was so
close she could feel the heat of his body and his breath
on her neck. But he did not touch her. "The glass."
She did and it must have been touch activated because
when her fingers met the cool glass it was as if a shade
lifted, and she could see inside the room. A woman was
crawling across the floor. All that she wore was a pink

collar on her neck attached to leather rope. She moved closer to the glass. At the other end of the rope stood a thick man. He was thick all over. His shoulders wide and it rippled with strength. He was fully clothed, but you could see every inch of him through the tight clothing he wore. His long locs hung below his shoulders. She was intrigued as she watched. The man had the woman to turn around, showing them her perfectly round derriere.

He swatted the woman's ass and Jericha gasped as she watched. He swatted her again and then he vigorously rubbed her cheeks. She could feel Jarohn watching her closely, but she couldn't turn away. Jarohn moved close to her again.

"Tell me what you are feeling?" "Ummm," she moans in response. "Words", he says again. "Do you think you could do something like this? And enjoy it? "Yes," she responds. "Does it turn you on?" She never knew something like this could, but it did. She shook her head before saying "yes". He cursed behind her before pressing pushing her up against the glass. "I don't know what it is about you. I've wanted you since I first seen you." He wrapped his arm around her from behind and spread her legs apart with his knee. "Would you let me take you right here?"

He could have taken her in the middle of the club, and she wouldn't have stopped him. She nodded her head and he pulled her by her hair sharply. "What did I say about using your words?" She stammered wincing at the sharp sting of her hair being pulled. He bit her neck from behind before smoothing it over with his tongue. She'd forgotten about the man and woman in the room until he whispered in her ear. Watch them. She opened her eyes, and the man was now behind the woman. They both were on the floor. He was still dressed except he must have had an open crotch because he was pounding in and out of her.

"Can they see us?" she asked. "What if they can? Would you stop me?" She surprised herself when she answered "no". She must have given him the answer that he wanted because he slowly peeled her jumpsuit from her skin. He left her feet tangled in its layers on the floor. She was naked beneath it. He inhaled sharply before touching her. "I want you to keep watching them. Don't close your eyes." It was nothing like she had ever experienced. It was raw, rough, and fast. When he was done, he told her to get dressed and follow him. He led her back upstairs to the room where they showered and this time, he made love to every inch of her. It was slow, meticulous, and perfect waking every inch of her body.

She later learned that it was not often that he touched the girls. He usually brought them to the club, employed them based on their looks or what he needed at the time. This ranged from receptionist, to bottle girls, strippers, call girls or anything that the club needed. The women brought the men which in turn brought more money. So, every girl was top of the line. A guy could have any flavor that he wanted. That night she went home with him and as promised he introduced her to a world of the unknown. It began all luxury, fantasy and fun but before she even realized it, it turned into terror, torture, and agony. He taught her how to please a man and he ignited a fire within her that would leave her stoking for days. He introduced her to BDSM and showed her how enjoyable pain and pleasure could be. But soon she found that inflicting pain seemed to pleasure him more. In the beginning she was eager to do anything he asked. His idea of intimacy and sex teetered on the edge of sadism. She had become his girl, his wife and slave. Before she knew it, she was trapped in that world that she was so eager to learn about. On the outside she was the perfect wife. Ironically, she had finished college. Jarohn had made sure that she did. She'd become an elementary school teacher. It was during school hours that she was able to live. She loved her students and secretly wanted kids of her own. But she could never bring a child into this world. Whenever, she walked out those school doors she had to prepare herself for her other life.

The first time she tried to leave, she reached out to her father in desperation. His only response was to hang up the phone up on her. It was then that she no longer felt fear, intimidation, or pain. She detached herself from that world mentally. She became numb to everything. She survived by separating her mind from what her body was experiencing. She had nothing else to give and couldn't allow herself to feel anything. The abuse became worse. Jarohn hated her because he wanted her so much. He would drink to try and erase her, but this only intensified his love and hate for her. In one night, he could confess his undying love for her, tell her how he craved her and could not get enough of her, then punish her for hours because he did. Three years had passed before she snapped out of it. Her mother came to her one night. She chastised her for becoming so weak. It had been so long since she had seen her. Jericha begged her mother to take her with her. She was through with this life. But instead, she woke from that dream with a renewed strength. Her mind would not allow her to vacate as she usually did. She felt every emotion. Her body vibrated with an anticipation that she did not understand. She could have killed him that day. She probably should have.

It was that night that she held his gun to his head. She wanted to pull the trigger so bad. But she didn't. But she fought back. She fought like hell with him and within herself. She wasn't sure what was worse, living with him or living with the constant internal struggle to return to what she knew. She picked up the phone many times to call him, just to hear his voice. She fought to understand the grip that one could have on a person. How she could still crave who she thought he was or could be though she knew he was not that man. How she tried to rationalize with herself that it may be better. Maybe he had learned his lesson after she had left. He could not help who his was. He did not intentionally hurt her. Who would ever want to be like that? But somehow, she fought this internal struggle. It was more of a battle between her mind and heart. It was the biggest hurdle that she had to overcome.

There was so much more to Jarohn's world. Creed was just a cover for the sex trafficking ring that he ran. He had enough money to make her disappear if he wanted her to. She was afraid to travel out of fear that he could track her. She'd abandoned her car in a mall parking lot and walked to a nearby side car lot, where she purchased herself another car cash. The owner didn't care who she was when she showed him the cash. Offering him a few more thousand dollars than what he was asking for. She stumbled across a private detective's office one night. After driving for hours, she was exhausted and couldn't keep her eyes opened any more. It was the only building down a dark dirt road. She'd pulled off the main roads in hopes of finding somewhere to crash for the night. The building was small. Old but it had a homey feel to it. She parked on the side of his office and fell asleep with the gun on her lap. She woke to a man knocking on her window. She felt for her gun. Released the safety and slowly looked up at the window. She was relieved when she didn't recognize the eyes peeking through the window. It wasn't Jarohn or anyone that she recognized from Creed. He raised his hands slowly when he saw the gun. "Hi, mam, are you ok? I promise I'm not here to hurt you." She placed the safety on the gun but kept it in her lap. She let down her window a few inches and apologized.

"I just needed a few hours of sleep. It was away from the road. I'm leaving now."

"You running from someone?" She shook her head no. But she could see the doubt and questions in his eyes. "You have something against hotels? Somehow you thought it would be safe to sleep in your car out here in the middle of nowhere?" "I kind of got lost. Thought I could drive through the night, but my eyes became heavy. My phone wasn't picking up service back here." That part was true since she had picked up a cheap prepaid phone.

"My names Jared" he had country drawl. Though he didn't look like any cowboy she'd ever seen. He motioned over his shoulder. She focused on the sign behind him. J Marshall. Personal Detective. The sign was small and plain. She was sure that she was in the same state because she hadn't passed any welcome to signs but she was 100s of miles away from Creed. The area brought on a sense of peace. From the time she turned down the small dirt road and pulled up next to the little white building a sense of peace and calm came over her as did the man that stood before her.

"Well, you might as well jump on out and come inside and get a cup coffee and stretch your legs before you take off." He showed her his badge and ID. "Take a picture of it if you want." She nodded her head and jumped out. A cup of coffee really did sound good right about now. She stretched and followed him inside. The inside reminded her of the inside of her grandparents' home. It was comfortable and homey. Secondhand furniture and a few pictures of different landscapes scattered the wall. An American flag was encased on the wall with several service medals and ribbons. She shared that cup of coffee with him and before she knew it, she had told him her life story. From her childhood, the loss of her mother, her father, Jarohn and Creed.

He listened intently. Didn't stop her once as she rushed to get it all out. When she was finished, she took a deep breath and finally looked up at him. "So now, what do you plan on doing with yourself now that you left that all behind?" he asked. "You wanna keep on running or your wanna keep fighting? Seems to me you still have a lot of fight in you left." She chose to fight. It took almost 2 years for them to build a case against Jarohn. Jared eventually went undercover. He began frequenting the club. On the outside it appeared to be just an upscale night club that catered to the elite. He did most of his research solo. Once he felt he had enough they took it to the authorities. Jared had connections on the force and brought it to one of his close friends that was still active.

Jericha stood in the club nervously. She knew that Jarohn would know that she was there. He was somewhere watching her. Nothing had changed. The same energy pulsed through the club and her. The many faces were different, some the same. She stood sipping on her drink. Waiting for him. It wasn't necessary that she came as Jared kept reminding her. But she knew that she had to. It was the only way that she could really feel free. Blue was there. She remembered him from her first night in Creed. He was the one that came for her tonight. She was still married to Jarohn and as far as they knew they were still together. She was sure Jarohn hadn't told anyone that she had left him. Blue greeted her.

"Mrs. Creed. It's been a while." She twisted her bracelet around her wrist. It was her mother's. It was one of the things her father had left for her in her room that first year when she would sneak in while he was gone. She rarely took it off. It was one of the few things she had left of her mother. "Mr. J said to see you up." She nodded and followed him though she knew the entire layout of the place. She had begun working there for Jarohn before they had married. But he did not like having her there and had quickly ended that. He was all for showing but not sharing. She followed Blue to Jarohn's office. She could have walked up there herself. But instead, she waited for him to send for her. Blue opened the door and closed it behind her after she walked into the office.

Jarohn was still handsome. But that was where the familiarity ended. Something was off about him. He lacked that confident air that he had about himself. He smiled when he saw her. "I knew you wouldn't be able to stay away for too long. How has life been treating you

Jericha?" Goose bumps ran up her arms at the sound of his voice.

"Life has been great," she paused "Jarohn." "Really? It couldn't have been anything like the life that I gave you," he gloated. "No" she shook her head. "It definitely has not been." He stood. "You really look great Jerri." He knew that she hated when he called her Jerri. It had been a mistake of telling him the name that her mother fondly called her by. In the beginning she had loved the way it sounded coming from his lips. It was comforting until he turned it into something ugly. She hated that he had even taken that away from her. She shook it off as he made his way towards her. She wanted to back away from him but instead she stood and waited for him.

"I've really missed you Jerri." He watched her for a response. "Tell me you've missed me too." "I can't say that I have" she answered. His eyes narrowed. She saw the flash of anger before he quickly recovered. "Are you ok?" She almost believed that he was genuinely concerned.

"I am." He sighed, "Ok get on with it then. If you aren't crawling your way back to me, then tell me exactly why you are here?" She took a step forward and he smiled in return reaching for her hand instinctively. She allowed him to touch her, though it made her skin crawl. He rubbed his thumb across her wrist. It was something else that she had loved him doing. That was until he showed her that those pressure points could be pleasurable and painful. He watched her intently. "What is it that you want from me? It can't be money because I know of the cash you hid. It should have been more than enough." She wasn't surprised that he knew of her stash. He did watch her every move. When she left that was the only thing that she had taken with her, and his gun. The authorities now had it tying him to several murders. She was sure that he searched for her. But with Jared's help she was able to take on a new identity.

She shrugged "I didn't…don't want to be running from you for the rest of my life. He kissed her hand and raising it to his face. "I wouldn't have come for you. I would have let you go. It isn't healthy to love you as much as I do. To crave you. His heated eyes digging into her. And oh, how I crave you." He turned away, "you did me a favor by leaving."

"Is that so?" She knew that he was lying because he did try for months to find her. She looked up at the clock that hung on his wall. She only had few minutes before they would be storming into his office. She knew that the cameras had already switched over as they raided the place. Everything appeared to be going as normal from his side. She wore the device on her bracelet that jammed his system along with a wire. She allowed him to bring her arms around his neck and hug her. It took everything her not to cringe from his touch. There was a time when she would melt in his arms whenever he touched her. Eventually she would stiffen at his touch and even that resolved into nothingness over time. Her reaction or lack thereof would always make him angrier. She learned how to retreat to nothingness as she did now. "I just wanted to say goodbye Jared."

"And you had to make a big production out of telling me goodbye? I thought you said bye when you

left the first time? With my gun pointed at my head?"
His eyes darkened.

She stepped out of his embrace and walked towards the door. It unlocked and for the first time a hint of confusion flashed across his face. She knew that his office was one of the rooms that he could controlled at his fingertips. She walked out of his office and met the SWAT team in the hall. One of them covered her with his shield and backed her into the hall and into the elevator where Jared was waiting for her. He checked from head to toe as she said barely audible, "He didn't hurt me. I'm ok." He breathed a sigh of relief letting go the air that he withheld in his lungs. Though she knew that he could hear their exchange. He must have needed proof because he kept checking for himself. He led her out of the building covering her when they heard gunshots. He ushered her into the waiting police car and told them to take her away.

She later learned that Jarohn had attempted to shoot himself in the head, but the officers stopped with a bullet in his shoulder. He didn't get to take the easy way out. He left Creed cuffed to a gurney. Jarohn was sentenced to life in prison. It had been 3 years since it all went down. She looked down at Jared who was now her husband. He held their daughter Essence. She looked so much like her mother. It had taken a long time for her to allow Jared past her barriers. He had waited until the case was over before he told her how he felt about her. It took another year before she allowed him to even touch her intimately. But he never gave up on her. For the first time ever, she experienced what it was to truly be loved by a man. To be adored by him. They had moved away to a small town called Beaufort in SC. It was a beautiful collection of islands where the natives spoke Gullah. Many of the roads were lined with huge oak trees that had grey tendrils hanging from its branches. She'd never known that such a place existed. Jared had told her that he had lived there years ago when he was a young corpsman in the Navy. When he retired from the Navy, he joined the police force. He had eventually left the police force to become a private detective though he still held close ties to both worlds.

He'd taken her there on vacation to Hilton Head which was another one of those islands. The beaches and little town were breathtaking. She had fell in love with the place and the people. She joined a local church and had introduced Jared to Christ. He joined shortly after and they had been praying and worshipping together and doing God's work. The old songs that the choirs sung reminded her of her mother so. Her and Jared had married in a private ceremony on Hilton Head. He built her a home on a small island called Cat Island and promised to spend every day of his life showing her how to enjoy life and to live it to its fullest. He kept his promise.

Treachery

So, how many women have always been the good girl? The good girlfriend? The perfect wife? The supermom???? And your man has yet to figure out how to appreciate it? He continues to cheat, lie, take you through baby momma dramas, having kids out of wedlock, sneaking, fucking, and sucking anything and everything in sight. Then comes home and expects a home-cooked meal, the house to be spotless, kids organized and ready for school, a shower, and you to then fuck him like his 20-year-old chic did last week. When does enough become enough? When is it your turn to have a little fun? To let down your hair, dance the night away, and not worry about a dozen calls and texts asking, where are you? Why are you not answering the phone? Then those texts eventually shifting to bitch I know you cheating! I knew you weren't shit! You better not bring your ass home tonight!

Yea you know all about it. But let me share with you my enough. How those messages slowly changed to baby are you alright? When are you coming home? Please don't leave me. I know I messed up. I can fix this. Please don't do this to us. I love you. What about our kids? Our home? Our family? Nigga please! Fuck you!

For the 5th weekend in a row, dinner is on the stove. Kids are upstairs asleep, and Lex is dozing on the sofa. Around 3 am the phone rings. Trey is on the line, "baby I'm on my way home. Are you still awake?" His speech is slurred. "Rome… Rome is bringing me home. Did you cook something to eat? Good because I'm starving." He's having a full-on conversation with himself because Lex has yet to respond. He rambles on and he signs off "be there in 2," then the dial tone. More pissed off that he had interrupted a good dream than the fact that it was 3 am and he wasn't home yet, Lex yawns and stretches. Several minutes, maybe hours later she hears the key in the door.

Trey stumbles in heading straight to jump in the shower yelling down the stairs "baby did you fix my plate?" It is an after-thought but funny that the slur in his voice is gone. He walks out in a towel a few minutes later. Strolls into the kitchen and grabs his plate. He looks back and smiles "mmmmh baby this smells good. My baby cooked for me! Baby, you're the best." He shimmies up like he's on the dance floor, placing a light kiss on her forehead, and does a slight jog up the stairs. He leans over and does a not-so-good job at whispering "come on up-stairs, let me touch something." Lex drags herself upstairs and curls up on her side of the bed.

"Thanks for waiting up for me." "Yeah, sure babe." Trey is trying to balance his plate and a beer, meanwhile, Lex was trying to balance her sanity, tears, and a headache. She needs to be up in another hour for work. After listening to the annoying sounds of lips smacking and the clang of his fork hitting the plate. Trey finally sighs, "damn that was good." Slurps down the last of his beer and is snoring by the time his head hits the pillow. His half-empty plate deserted on the floor beside the bed along with his other collections of snack bags and trash.

The next day's work is hell. Her 12-hour shift turns into 16. By 8:30 pm, Trey is calling. She sends a quick text when she dips into the break room. "Working a double don't get off until 10 tonight." Lisa had once again called in. Hell, Lisa seems to call in every shift that Lex works.

Or she is running late. Lex takes a second in the break room to slip off her shoes and rub her feet. Mid yawn Tracy walks in. "Hey, love. I know you are tired. They called me and asked me to come in early so that you can get out of here. You're already in overtime as usual." Lex quickly does turn over and heads home.

As she pulls into the driveway, she notices that Trey's car isn't parked as usual. She unlocks that door and walks in. The house is quiet and there's a note on the counter. Trey's handwriting is scribbled in blue ink, out with the fellas, the kids are at your mom's! See you later. Dishes are strewn all over the kitchen and the living room. She sighs. Thinks fuck this. Takes a shower and calls it a night. Saturday morning crawls in with the sunlight peeping between the shades. As she stretches, she notices that Trey's side is empty. She reaches on the nightstand and checks her phone and of course, there's a message. Baby, did you make it home yet? I had a little too much to drink. Staying over to Rome's. See you tomorrow. I love you. This occurs at least twice a month.

Lex and Trey have been together since high school. Lex was quiet in school. She stayed to herself and only had one close friend, her best friend Lisa. She and Lisa were friends for as long as she could remember. Trey was an all-star in school playing basketball, football and he ran track. He wasn't the best-looking guy on the team but what he lacked in looks his smile and body made up for. His smile was perfect, and he would often throw one Lex's way. He and

Lex's brother Tye were best friends. She was more of a little sister to Trey but eventually, that little sister grew up. She had curves for days.

Trey hid his feelings during his sophmore and junior years. But it wasn't long before he began losing interest in the cheerleaders and step team girls that he was used to dating and dropping. He started spending more of his time watching Lex from a distance. Lex was smart, cute, and had a body that would have a guy begging to touch. During the summer of graduation, Tye left for boot camp and Lex was home alone often.

It was then that the chemistry changed between them. Trey kept coming around, though Tye was away. He would mow the lawn for her mom, and he'd show up for dinner on the pretense that he was looking out for Tye's mom and little sister. Lex was a senior. She only needed a few credits so she would be graduating after the first semester. She would then continue at the local college so that she could also work and help her mother out.

One afternoon Trey stopped by lightly tapping on her window. Lex peaked through the shades, opened the door, and walked back into the living room. Trey followed behind slowly. Lately, he was uncomfortable being alone with Lex, but that didn't stop him from checking in on her. Their mom was always working. She taught middle school at the local Junior High during the day and nights and in summers she worked housekeeping. Lex was lounging in one of those little shorts and a tank thing she loved to wear. She never knew the effect she had on him when she wore those things. She had legs for days that lead to wide hips and a small waist.

Lex was 17, she'd be 18 in a few weeks.

"So, what do you have planned for your birthday?"
"Nothing. I have to study so that I can graduate early." She rambled on about some physics test she had coming up. She dual studied at the college and was already taking classes towards her nursing degree. Trey was focused on her smooth legs curled up on the all-white sofa. Their home was always clean. You could eat off the floor. Someone had to be just a little OCD because the house was spotless. The furniture was white and there was never a stain on the carpet or furniture. You left your shoes on the small shoe rack at the door when you entered. His gaze continued up her legs to her thighs before resting at the hem of her shorts. He fantasized about touching her, as his gaze trailed up her arm, neck and rested on her lips. She smiled as she tilted her head her lips forming his name. "Trey" she sang as she often did. Her words always

came out sounding like open mike night at the poetry hall. Or she often spoke in a melody whenever she became excited. She called out "Trey" again, "are you even listening to me?"

He smiles in return because she's smiling. "Yes, Lex, I am." Though his mind was away in some land where he and Lex were making out, he could still repeat what she was saying. He was very good at multitasking, as over the years he learned to tune out what was going on around him while still being keenly aware of what was going on. It was a survival strategy he'd learned growing up in foster care. Absently his answers "Yes baby, I heard everything you said." Caught off guard Lex grimaces. If he hadn't been watching her, he may have missed it, because she quickly recovered and smiles shyly "baby?" She throws a pillow at him. "Gross Trey! I am not one of those little chicken head cheerleaders you be chasing behind!" The pillow bounced off his forehead.

He stands as he considered jumping on the couch with her and tickling her until she yelled mercy as he always did. But he knew that if he did, he wasn't sure if he'd be able to stop himself from doing something foolish. She braced for his retaliation anyway, however, he walked over to her with a goofy grin on his face. Alright kiddo, I gotta head out. Have you gotten any letters from Tye this week? He saw the sadness in her eyes when he mentioned her brother. She nods her head "no".

Tye had left home for boot camp upset. He and their mom had argued that night about him going into the military. It wasn't safe their mom would always say. I don't want you to go off to fight no war for a country that could care less about you. He left out the next morning without waking any of them to say goodbye. He left sealed envelopes on the table for her and her mom. He'd left one in her room for Trey as well with instructions for her to give it to him. She looked down at the carpet fibers counting them in her head. Trey lifted her chin saying, "no worries, I'm sure he's getting his ass whooped and hasn't had a chance to yet, or who knows, maybe he isn't allowed to write letters just yet. "I know he's thinking of ya'll and misses you."

She nodded her head again. "I gotta go kiddo," he says again. More so because of where his thoughts were leading him. "I'll see you around", she mumbles.
He leaned in and kissed her forehead, something he'd always done. However, this time he lingered longer, inhaling her scent. She stiffened before immediately relaxing, reminding

herself that this was Trey. However, her forehead tingled long after he was gone.

Lex had a crush on Trey for as long as she could remember, but Tye would have killed them both. It was during middle school that she started noticing that he was just as uncomfortable around her as she. He'd kissed her once freshman year when her boyfriend had broken up with her. They had only dated for a few weeks before he'd dumped her because she wasn't putting out as he put it. She was walking home alone and spotted Trey walking opposite her after skipping his afternoon classes. He jogged up to her asking "what's wrong kiddo and why the hell are you walking alone?"

She shrugged her shoulders and wiping away her tears. "Hey, are you crying? What wrong?" He walked beside her in silence for a moment. They slowed as they came closer to her house. He pulled her into the trail that he and Tye often snuck girls. He led her to their fort that they played in many summers and winters. It wasn't really a fort. It was a small clearing in the woods that they had dragged an old couch and table to.

The trees were thick all around it creating their imaginary shack. He was walking backward. "Are you gonna talk to me? What happened?" he asked again. He walked up to her, his shadow covering her. "Phillip broke up me", her lips quivered. He lifted her chin as he so often did. "Good", he caught himself.

Anger coursing through him. The idiot had no right anyway. She was too smart to be fooling with him anyhow. "Did he do anything to you," he asked? She shook her head. "No, he just said no one wanted a prissy ass, stuck up little bitch who didn't put out." "He said what?!" Shhhh, she whispered loudly. "That little shit!" "Watch your mouth" she snarled. "I didn't allow him to speak to me that way and I won't allow you either."

He paused, "now there goes my girl." He smiled, "are you really surprised or even really hurt? Why would you even waste your time with him?" What he wanted to say was "I thought you were waiting for me?" "No worries, I'm gonna beat the shiii…" he glanced up, "mess out of him when I see him." "No need, I slapped him when he called me a bitch."

"That a girl kiddo." Thunder pounded in the sky and out of nowhere the rain flooded the sky. Laughing they ran under the canopy that the trees created. Her hair had begun to curl. "Dang it, I spent hours straightening this mess, it didn't forecast rain this week" she pouted. He reached out and touched her hair. "I like it better curly anyways." Without thinking she leaned over and kissed him on the lips. They paused lips to lips, and he closed his eyes. Willing himself to be still. She kissed him again. Just a light brush of lips but It felt like lightning had struck him. He backed away into the rain. Letting the water soak him. He shook his head trying to clear it. She stood watching him.

"You sure you're ok he asked?" She shook her head yes. "I'm sorry, I don't know what I was thinking. Then again, yes, I did. I wanted my first kiss to be with you". She smiled. "I had to see what all the fuss was about and... it was nice," her smile widening. She turned and walked away. He stood there long after she was gone, the downpour only lasted a few minutes, before fading to a light mist. He listened for her door to open and close. Their house was just on the other side of the trees.

"Oh shit, I'm in trouble" he shook his head with a smile on his face. Trey woke from his dream. He was dreaming again about his and Lex's first kiss. He stretched and turned. Tanya was lying next to him sleeping peacefully. He needed to stop this shit. He knew that he didn't really deserve Lex. He didn't even know why the hell he was here. Easing out of the bed, he crept quietly, grabbed his clothes, dressed quickly, and slipped out of the house. Damn. He had fallen asleep to Tanya's place again. Trey met Tanya at his gym.

She had a thing for him from day one. As most ladies did. Tanya was slightly overweight but determined to lose it. She went hard over the next few months and had toned up nicely. She was cute. She wore a short haircut. Her dark skin smooth, reminding him of cocoa. She was one of the few that he double dipped. He usually didn't linger long with any female, but she kept coming back for an encore and he obliged.

Over the years Trey had grown into his looks, as they say. His skin was dark and stretched tightly over his muscular body. His teeth were perfect. His eyes were just as dark as his skin, a piercing dark brown that was almost black.
He'd spent years training and created a body these women worship. It was only natural that he would become a personal trainer. It was a way to stay in shape and he got an assortment

of women that would come through day after day. His gym was a blessing and a curse.

The gym was his dream. Though, it was Lex's smart mind and sacrifice that brought his dream to life. She worked hard while going to school, having their babies, and helping him build an empire. They now owned 3 gyms in the Atlanta area. They had left the comfort of country living in the Low-country and had moved to Atlanta to pursue their dreams. They started out in a small studio apartment. Lex had taken a job as a new grad at a Level 3 Trauma center. She became a nurse and worked her way up to nursing supervisor. She ran a tight ship in the mother-baby unit. Perhaps that's what ignited her baby fever. For the first few years, she was pregnant every year. She worked nights so that she would be home with the kids during the day. Trey stayed home for the first few years helping around with the kids while hitting the gym in the afternoons offering personal training. Lex stayed fit because they pushed one another. She was his first protégé. Hell, she was his first everything. He did love her. He just enjoyed the attention of all women as well.

Lex had graduated from high school with honors. Tye was away at his first duty station and they talked almost daily. She was missing him like crazy. He asked about college, Trey, who was getting into a lot of trouble and what was going on in their little hometown. Trey had injured his knee playing college ball and was in a funk about it. He was sitting around drinking himself into a state of depression. Something he'd suffered with off and on since childhood. He was bitter and angry. Their roles had reversed. She was the one now checking on him. At the time she was a certified nursing assistant and working at one of the local nursing homes. She'd often stop and pick him up something to eat and drop in on him. He hated the physical therapist that came to see him. He hated physical therapy and everything else. He would often refuse to do any of the exercises that the therapist encouraged him to do.

"I'm worried about him Tye, she said, "he's not himself." "What he needs is a strong woman. Not these damn airheads he likes running through. I thought for sure you two would have been dating by now." "What" Lex questioned. "Man, you must not be getting any sleep. Why would I ever date Trey?"

"You think I didn't know ya'll had a thing for each other. He slipped and told me about you kissing him. He was half-drunk and kept apologizing, swearing he never would hit on my kid sister. But I knew better. I saw how ya'll would watch each other when you thought no one was watching. Don't try to tell me he hasn't made a move on you when I left for boot camp." She stuttered "he didn't!"

"How do you think I was able to leave you and mom when I did? I knew that Trey would look after you guys. I made him promise that he would." Lex had pondered on their conversation for days. Ok, so if Tye didn't care then what was stopping her. She liked Trey. She really thinks that she's in love with him. If they did get together then he and Tye could be brothers for real. She never had a problem going after what she wanted. And hell, Trey was something she had wanted for a long time.

She stopped by his place on her way home. He was staying in the projects on 5th street. Yes, even little old Savannah Georgia had projects. She was always nervous coming through there, but he lived in the entrance of the apartments. She'd always call or text if she were gonna stop by. She had learned her lesson of just showing up when she walked in on him with another girl. She could hear their screams and moans from the hall. She had to admit that it turned her on. She always wanted him to be her first. She had heard in the halls and locker room how great he was in bed in their high school days. She had her own key to his place and would sometimes stop in and straighten up for him. They would hang out some days and she had even stayed over. He'd give her his bedroom and crash on the couch. Especially if one of her mom's guy friends was over there.

They always had wondering eyes. A few of them had hit on her when her mom wasn't there. She shook her head. She wasn't even going down that road today. She knocked before letting herself in. Trey was hobbling trying to make it to the door. "Go sit down."

She could tell that he was in pain. She sniffed at the air "ugh, no wrong direction." Bathroom, now. She handed him his crutches. "What good are they if they are leaned up against the wall?" He limped, crutched to the bathroom. She had run ahead of him and turned on the shower. She had her supply kit in her bag. She grabbed out what she needed and bagged his knee. She tossed him a washcloth and towel. "I'd prefer a sponge bath" he grumbled. "Boy, I wish I would! How about you call me if you need a hand" she closed the door. She changed the channel and settled on the couch. After about 20 minutes she called out to Trey "You ok in there?" No answer. She stood and walked down the hall.

"Trey you ok?" she rapped on the door. She pushed it open. He was sitting on the floor of the shower with his head down. "I'm fine he snapped. I just caught a damn cramp. Shut my door." "Trey?" "Leave me alone Lex!" Like hell.

Anger quickly replaced her concern. "Get your ass up! Up sick of this shit! Get up before I drag you up my damn self." "Leave me the fuck alone Lex!" he yelled punching the wall. His eyes were red, she wasn't sure if he had been crying or if it was because the shower water was running in his eyes He had his hand covering himself.

"Unless you wanna see something else I suggest you close my door." She stood with her hands on her hips. "Boy please, you ain't got nothing I ain't already seen and handled." He raised an eyebrow, forgetting that he was on the shower floor. He challenged her, his eyes darkening. "Exactly what have you seen and handled Lex?" "Stand and maybe I'll show you."

With ease and little effort, he reached up and lifted himself. She kept her eyes level with his. He continued to stare at her. His hands lifted above him bracing his weight on both sides. She glanced down quickly, swallowed, and looked off. "See something you like? Don't look away now. You were all mouth a few minutes ago." His eyes sparkled devilishly. "You sure about handling all of this?" he leaned forward. standing confidently. Her interpretation of handling was more on the lines of her job. She could drop a catheter in with ease. That was about the most of handling anything she'd experienced. But he didn't have to know that.

"Maybe" she shrugged her shoulders as if unaffected. Either way, it worked getting him out of his funk and got him off the shower floor. "Make your way into the living room and I may have to show you."

She left out and went to the kitchen. She made him a quick sandwich and grabbed a coke. He crutched in with just a towel wrapped around him and sat on the chair.

She noticed his face tightened as he eased down onto the couch, his injured leg up in the air. "Did you take your meds," she asked? "You know I don't like taking that shit." His parents were addicted to all kinds of drugs, so he refused to take any form of narcotics.

"Well, don't you have some 800 mgs?"

She walked over to him and handed him the plate, tossed him a bag of chips, and set the coke on the table beside him. She sank in the chair next to him. "I'm sorry for snapping at you earlier, this shit sucks and hurts like a bit-, he sighs it just hurts." She rummaged through the assorted bottles on the table grabbing the Ibuprofen. She shook out one and handed it to him. "I'm good", he says. "No, you're not, take the Motrin Trey." He turns to her, his eyes glinting again. "Ok, let me see it." She holds out her hand, palms up. He reaches for her hand and lifts it to his mouth. She stiffens, as he kisses her fingers watching her. "Put it in my mouth." "Quit playing boy", she says shakily.

He watches her squirm becoming more and more uncomfortable. "Relax Lexi," he only calls her Lexi when he's trying to calm her. "It's just me", he says. She tries to pull away but he's still holding her hand. He lifts it to his mouth again. Takes the pill into his mouth and kisses her palm again. He grabs for the coke with his other hand without breaking eye contact and takes a sip. He kisses her hand again. "You want to take the pain away?" he asked.

"Of course," she says without a second thought. "I hate to see you in pain. Physical pain, mental pain. I know your hurting, but I need you to push through this." Tears formed in her eyes, "I need you to be my big brother, I need you to be strong Trey. Or else I won't have anyone. Tye already left me. I know you're here physically, but I can't help but feel I'm losing you too." "I'm right here," he says gently. "I haven't left you." He lifts her chin and wipes away a tear.

"Don't do this Trey.

It took you so long to come out of the last one. I need you," she sniffles. "Don't let this destroy you. I know you had plans of playing pro but it's not the end of the world. You're talented and smart. There are other things you can do, like coaching." She lays her head on his shoulder. Her emotions were all over the place because she was concerned about him, but it also wasn't going as she planned. He leans his head against hers and traces her fingers with his. There were many days they hung out and laid around just like this. It was time to change it up. She didn't want to be his friend or little sister.

She knew he wanted her but out of respect for her brother had held back. She lifts his hands and kisses his fingers one at a time. It was his time to freeze.

"What the hell? Lex, what do you think you are doing?" He pulls his hand away and sits up. Shaking his head, he looks up at her. Her face was serious, but he could tell that she was nervous. She leans forward and kisses him. He takes in a deep breath.

"Woah. What the fuck Lex?" He lets his breath out shakily Lex?" "Trey? she looks down whispering "I want you to be my first." "First? First what Lex?" She looks up at him

again and tries to look back down quickly, but he stops her.
He holds her in place with his palm at the side of her face.
He stares at her, looks down at her lips, and back up into her
eyes. His voice deepening. "Lex…" Before she could change
her mind, she leans in and kisses him again. It was the first
time they'd kissed since that day in the 9th grade. Again, she
is the one that initiated it. She tries to pull back, but he
deepens the kiss. Inside her thoughts are going a mile a
minute. What the hell are you doing Lex? But his lips are so
soft. Should I be enjoying a kiss this much? She leans into
him more. She'd kissed other guys before. She'd even come
close several times, but she would always stop them. Trey
explored her mouth reaching down he trails his fingers
against her skin peeking from under her cropped top.
She wore another one of those tanks and shorts sets, but this
time her cropped top exposed her flat stomach. When he
pulls back, she tries to slow her breathing.

He was staring at her lips again. He leaned his
forehead against hers. "Lex, we better stop while I can," he
says. "I don't want you to stop." She may be nervous, but she
knew without a doubt that she did not want him to stop.

"I want this Trey. I want you," she swallowed. "But you just said your first. You mean to tell me you've never?" she shakes her head. "Damn Lex. I can't!" "Sure, you can."

She reaches down wanting to touch him. She felt him thicken beneath the towel. He grabs her hand stilling her touch. Then wraps her hand around him and rubs her hands up and down the length of him. She felt him harden more. He watches her the entire time. He leans his head back on the couch and closes his eyes. "Keep touching me." She continues to explore him. Wondering how he felt beneath the towel. When she paused, he sat up. He reaches for her and kisses her roughly. He breaks contact only long enough to remove her shirt. "Touch me again," he says.

This time she grips him beneath the towel. He lifts his hips and removes the towel. She likes how he felt, his skin smooth over steel. She hesitantly grips him. He moans. "Stand up." She does without hesitation.

"Damn I'm going to enjoy this more than I should. Take your clothes off." She does and stands before him. She thought she'd be shy but the way he looked at her only emboldened her. "Come here." She moves closer to him. He grips her waist and trails kisses down her stomach. He lifts her onto his lap. He kisses her again, explores her mouth, lips, neck, and breast.

At this point, all thoughts are gone. He rubs himself against her. "Your gonna have to ride me, baby. If I could, I would." She looks at him confused. "Oh, maybe once you're all healed?" "Like hell!" He shifts his hips to lay back on the sofa, carrying her with him. "Come here" he whispers, kiss me." She leans forward and does so. The kiss is intoxicating. She forgets everything as he moves her against him building a slow rhythm. "Move with me, yes just like that."

He continues giving commands and she follows his lead. Between their kisses, he tells her how much she means to him. How beautiful she is. How it was always her. How much he needed her. He entered her slowly giving her time to adjust to him and controlled the pace gripping her hips. He told her how he couldn't believe that she was finally his. He took his time until the discomfort turned to pleasure. When they were done, she laughed "Damn if I knew it was going to be like that, I would have done this a long time ago."

They stayed up all night talking. "Damn I sure hope Tye don't trip too much, because there is no way this is only going down once." She told him the details of her and Tye's conversation and he laughed. "Man, I was hooked a long time ago. There was no way he didn't know. But I tried like hell to act like I didn't have a thing for you. Look at you. Who wouldn't?"

"You're gorgeous, smart, any man would be lucky to have a woman like you. Well, would have been lucky, because your all mine now." She blushed. "I know how you are Trey. We don't have to make anything official. I wanted that experience with you, and it was amazing. Which I knew it would be."

"Oh, and it will continue to be amazing because it's going to happen again, and again and again. Matter of fact it's about to happen in the very near future." He leaned down and kissed her. The second time around was even better than the first. He told her that he loved her. That he had always loved her. He vowed that day to be there for her and to go hard in everything in life so that he could be a better man. Not only for her but for himself. He told her that it was mind over matter and that he would not only fight physically but mentally as well.

Trey Jr. was conceived on that day. This only pushed him more. She was just what he needed. He attacked physical therapy aggressively, and after completing PT he worked just as hard in the gym. Rebuilding his muscle strength and doubling his muscle mass. The gym became an addiction. He dabbled in selling dope for a little while but after finding out that Lex was pregnant, he quickly ditched that. He couldn't be locked up anywhere and leave his son without a father. So, he got a job at the nearby gym. He started out cleaning up the place. He would work out in the evenings when things were quiet. It was a 24-hour gym, and he was allowed 1 hour to work out during his shift.

Trey proposed to Lex in the delivery room while she was in labor with Trey Jr (JT). He promised her that he would never let them down and that he was going to be the best father that he could ever be. At least he kept that promise. He was the best father. But he continued to let her down repeatedly. She graduated with her a practical nursing degree before having JT. A year later she obtained her associate degree in nursing. After that, they moved into a small two-bedroom apartment in Atlanta.

Trey obtained his certification as a personal trainer. He worked in gyms in Atlanta training others how to discipline their bodies and change not only their physical appearance but their lifestyle. He went to school and studied physical therapy while she worked and cared for the kids. He eventually graduated as a physical therapist. The two of them worked hard to get to where they were. That was the start of their problems. School, work, and children left little alone time for them. With reward came sacrifice and their marriage suffered. Their sex life changed drastically from several times a week to several times a month.

She was always too tired or busy and these women at the gym were begging for his attention. It wasn't long before conversation became personal, and these women were bold. It wasn't long before he was giving more than lessons at the gym. The first time he cheated he felt bad. He thought for sure his guilt showed. He came home wanting to be the dotting husband. He brought flowers and tried to seriously tell her how much he loved her.

She waved him off, telling him that she loved him too. Over time the cheating came easy. He knew it was wrong but, what she didn't know couldn't hurt her. But she did know. Longer than he thought. As she had put it, he couldn't keep his little hoes on a tight leash. Some boldly approached her thinking that if they told her about their relationship that she would leave him. Others smirked in her face, giving off hints that she'd better hold on to her man because if she couldn't they sure as hell would. She threw herself into her work more after finding out. Trying to run away from her problems. She'd pick up any extra shifts just to avoid being home. She refused to let him touch her. On the outside, they were the perfect couple but deep down the pain was more than she could bear. Every woman wanted her life. Yet, she only wanted out.

She'd been the perfect wife and never looked at another man. She worked hard, kept a clean home, made sure dinner was cooked, or ordered depending on the day. Either way, a hot meal was always on the table when he got home. She worked hard to save money so that he could open his gym. But the more successful they became, the more they grew apart.

Lately, he was out late every night and gone most weekends. Well, since he was at Rome's again and the kids were with her mom, she decided it was time for her to have a little fun too. She sat up and sent her mom a quick text. *Do you mind keeping the kids for the weekend? No problem* her mom responds. She was off for the next 2 days so what the hell. She got up took a shower and headed out. First stop was to the nail shop. She didn't get her nails done often because she couldn't wear them long at work. However, she settled for a short set in a nude color. As she jumped in the car, she called Lisa. "Hey friend what are you up to this weekend?"

"Nothing girl, bored as usual. What are you up to?" "Come up here and see me. I miss my bestie!" "Girl Trey must have dropped off the face of the earth!" "Something like that." She paused for a second holding back tears. "I really need you to come," Lisa picked up on the change in her voice. "What's wrong? What the hell did he do?" Lex tries to smile and lighten her tone. "Nothing girl, I just missed you. I'm off this weekend and mom has the kids. I thought we could hang out." Without hesitation, Lisa says, "ok I'll be there in few hours." Lisa still lives in Savannah. Which is about 3 hours away. Lex turns the music up and heads to the hair salon. She is sure her stylist is booked, but it isn't often that she can get her hair done. She is sure she will fit her in. She ended up having to wait an hour but that was ok. Lisa had texted her and said she was on the way. She headed to the counter and decided to get a 30-minute massage while she waited then decided that she might as well get the package.

This included a massage, facial, hair, and makeup. By the time she was done Lisa had texted that she almost there. Lex headed home pulled in the driveway at the same time as Lisa. "Damn girl what did I miss? No scrubs. You beat for the gods! Yea something's up. Don't tell me you done killed this nigga and hid the body or some shit?" "Girl no! Shush that noise. I just needed to get out of this funk and treat myself for a change." "Ok, so what are we doing tonight? "My thoughts exactly!" They head into the house.

Trey was lounging on the couch. "Where have you been all day? I thought you were at work." She rolls her eyes at him as Lisa trails in behind her. "Hey Trey!" "Aw hell naw! What you doing here?" He stands and gives her a quick hug. In his mind, he really is trying to figure out what the hell she was doing here. He looks at Lex and does a double take. He kisses her "you look good, better than good." He slaps her on the ass. Now, why the hell she gonna get all dressed up and have Lisa come over here. It had been a while since he felt that pull to her like this. He was trying to figure out what was different about her.

"Lisa, girl make yourself at home," she says. "Trey, can you put her things in the guest room, she's staying for the weekend." Lisa laughs "Biyatch what guess room, ya'll know that's my damn room!" He goes out to the car and grabs Lisa's bag out of the trunk and takes it upstairs to the guest room. He hears Lex yell down "Lisa I'll be right back girl" and heads into their bedroom.

He follows her into the room. "Hey babe, sorry about last night." "I really do need to slow up a little. I'm getting too old for this shit and can't handle that liquor like I used to. What you and Lisa up to today?" She shrugs her shoulders. "I don't know. Mom's gonna keep the kids for the weekend so I called her to hang out." "Damn and you had to get all fine to hang out with Lisa? What about me?" She looks back at him. "What about you?" "If I knew we were gonna be kids free for the weekend, we could have hung out together." He creeps up behind her wrapping his arms around her. "I miss you, baby." He starts rubbing his hands between her legs and kissing her neck. He pushes her up against the wall and nudges the door shut with his foot. He's instantly hard and fiddles with the zipper on the back of his dress. She tries to pull away.

"Ummm, you don't know what you do to me baby coming up in here looking and smelling all good." She melts under his touch as he reaches under her dress and pulls her panties to the side dipping his fingers inside of her.

"Mmmm baby you all wet just for me?" Something about the fact that Lisa was downstairs turned him on more. "Damn I need you baby." Stay right there. He locks the door and undresses in record time. "Spread your legs. She does as he asks, and he slips inside of her. He reaches around her and grips her neck, gently but with just enough pressure. He knows that this turns her on. She really did miss him. The sex was fast and wild. She kept trying to shush him so that Lisa couldn't hear them but the more she tried to be quiet the harder he pounded her from behind. "Your mines right baby? Say it" She heard the tv turn on and the surround sound got louder. She was sure Lisa could hear them. He slows down his rhythm. "Damn baby I love you. You feel so damn good." She leans over gripping her knees so she could get down on him like he likes. She knew how to make him finish in seconds if she wanted. That's why she couldn't understand why he hey kept stepping out on her.

Blocking those thoughts from her mind, she focuses on pleasing her husband. A few strokes later he is trembling and whispering, "damn baby I'm almost there…what about you?" He slows then speeds up and slows again. A few minutes later they both are leaning against the wall trembling. She dashes away tears and heads into the restroom. He follows her. "That was good baby." He looks up in the mirror behind her. She ducks her head but not before he sees the tears. He turns her around. "What's wrong? I know it was good, but it didn't last long enough for you to be in tears." He smiles.

She forces herself to smile back. "Nothing. I don't know. I've been a little emotional lately. I think I just need a break." He hugged her.

"You do work too hard. I've been trying to tell you that for years. You don't need to you know. We have enough money for you to go part-time or not work at all." "I'm fine really. I just need a vacation to kind of reset." "You know I love you right?" "Yea, I know. She steps into the shower shutting the door. "So, it's like that. I can't join you, huh?" "No sir, you ain't messing up my hair or make-up. I will only be in for a few minutes. You can jump in right after me."

She hears the sink faucet turn. "I'll just wash up in here really quick." She waits until he leaves out of the bathroom before getting out of the shower. She looks at herself in the mirror. Thinking to herself, what am I doing wrong. Why isn't this enough? She was thankful for the waterproof makeup and didn't have to do much to touch it up. She shoots Lisa a text.

Sorry girl. Had to handle business.

Now he'll sleep for a few hours.

Go get dressed. Club attire.

Meet you downstairs in an hour.

She walks into their walk-in closet and picks out a cute jumper. It hugs her curves but isn't too revealing. Hell, she had to get out of the house and didn't need Trey's ass trying to follow them out. Trey was snoring lightly in the bed. Good, she thought. She threw on some matching shoes and went downstairs. Lisa was dressed cute in a black lace romper and heels. She had curled her waist-length hair and her make-up was on point.

"Damn we look good," they laughed and posed like they were on the runway. They hadn't hung out in a long time and planned on having a good time! They decided on a paint and sip spot that she had always to try out but never had time. It was a nice way to start the evening. The two of them were feeling nice after a few glasses of wine. But their paintings were wall worthy. She loved the African-themed turbans that they painted. They put their portraits in the car and decided to call an Uber. They headed to the strip and grabbed a bite to a nice little pub and caught up like old times. Afterward, they bar hopped and ended the night at one of the local nightclubs. It was a 25 and older spot so it wasn't full of teenyboppers. They were at the bar again, feeling quite tipsy when two guys approached them.

"Hey, ladies, ya'll are sure having a good time. Let us get your next set of drinks." They looked at each other and cracked up. "Sure!" they chimed together. They sat next to them and chatted for a while. Lex made sure to tell them that they both were married and just hanging out together. Though she was the only one married. She didn't want them getting any ideas of how their night was ending. But this didn't deter them. The four of them ended up on the dance floor and she and Lisa partied like they were in college again. Their names were Bret and Brenden. They were brothers and said that they were out doing the same. Bret was in town from New York and he and Brenden were catching up. Both were cute but Brenden was fine. A couple of times he pulled Lex a little too close and she had to keep putting space between them. But the drinks were flowing, and he smelled nice. Lisa excused them pulling her away into the restroom.

"Girl Trey gonna kick your ass! You know ya'll like damn mini celebrities around here. What the hell do you think you're doing?" Lex sway slightly. "I ain't doing nothing! We just having a little fun!" "Yeah right, it's time to go. We've had enough fun for one night. Shit one week. I already called us an uber." They walked back through the club. Lisa tried going around the other side to miss the brothers, but Lex caught Brenden's eye and waved at him. They followed them asking to walk them to their car.

"We have an Uber coming. Matter of fact they'll be pulling up in a second" Lisa said glancing down at her phone. Brenden reached for Lex's hand and twirled her around. "Your husband is a very lucky man. He's also a fool for letting you out all alone tonight. You sure you don't want us to give ya'll a lift?"

"Oh no, hell no," Lisa said. "Thank you for a great evening fellas. But there goes our ride." As they were jumping into the backseat Lex glanced back smiling and blew Brenden a kiss. He yelled back "Now see you play too much." He tapped his lips. "I prefer the real deal." He was too cute to pass up. She felt like having some more fun. Lex turned around and ran back up to him. What the hell. She stood on her tippy toes and kissed him. It was just a quick peck, but it ran straight through her. He smiled handing her his card. "You should call me some time." "I just might" she laughed and ran back to the truck. "Oh yea, I see we gonna be in jail. Because Trey gonna try to kill your ass and then we gonna have to kill him" Lisa grumbled. "Trying to get my ass in trouble. Naw. No mam. I'm taking your ass straight home! Orange is not my color."

"Evening ladies," the driver said. "Evening to you." Lex leaned over the seat. "It must be my lucky night. All the fellas are cute. I'm Lexi." "Your night is over mam and alcohol makes everyone cute." The driver frowns. "No offense to you," Lisa says. "You sir are very cute, and she is very married. Can you handle getting us home?" "Sure thing."

Trey reached for his phone once again. Only 15 minutes had passed since he last checked it. Where in the hell were Lex and Lisa? He'd texted her hours ago to ask when she would be home. It went unread along with the string of other texts he'd sent. He lifted the glass to his lips and took a sip. He had lost count after the first few. Leaning back in his chair he flipped the channels again. He was supposed to go out tonight as well but had changed his mind.

Tanya had hit him up, but he was spent, after the loving Lex had put on him earlier, he wasn't sure he could live up to round two. He sat up when he thought he'd heard a car pull up. Several minutes later Lex and Lisa stumbled in the door giggling. "Shhh, Lex whispered loudly, before you wake Trey." "Bitch you ain't being quiet your damn self" as they broke out into another fit of giggles. "Oh, hey babe did we wake you" Lex sashayed towards him.

Lisa made a beeline for the guest room. "Night you two lovebirds!" His wife leaned forward to kiss him and toppled face-first into his lap. She giggled some more, smacking her lips. She put her fingers to her lips and whispered to his lap. "Shhh we wouldn't want to wake the man, now would we?" After several attempts at unbuttoning his pants, she gave up and curled in his lap. She kissed him smelling of alcohol and mumbled something about him being lucky she was turning down fine ass niggas for his bitch ass. Not long too long after she was snoring softly. He kissed her on the forehead, wrinkling in thought. But he shrugged it off, lifted his wife, and headed upstairs. She was gonna be pissed in the morning because she hadn't washed that makeup off her face. But she was too cute to wake. Lex didn't usually drink, and it had been years since she went out.

Lex woke to the heavyweight of Trey wrapped around her. She tried stretching but gave up with Trey tangled around her. She dreamed of Brenden's smile and kiss, among other things. She tried shaking the image from her head but that caused the room to spin and her pound head. "Argghh hell", she whispered.

She quietly untangled Trey from her limb by limb and went into the bathroom. She rummaged around in the cabinet until she found a bottle of aspirin. Took 2 and cupped a handful of water from the sink. She looked up into the mirror. Her face was a mess, with her day-old makeup smeared and her hair already thickening and curling up. She sighed turning the water on, waited until the water was warm, and jumped into the shower.

She leaned against the shower wall allowing the water to run down her face and hair. A few seconds later she felt the temperature in the air shift as Trey eased in. He shot her a smile, "hey babe". She couldn't help but smile in return. He kissed her. One thing led to another and before she knew it her legs were wrapped around his shoulders. After he was done pleasing her, he lowered her and wrapped her legs around his waist. Woah, twice in 2 days, they were hitting records. Afterward, he washed her hair and then her from head to toe. She stepped out onto the fluffy mat outside the shower and toweled off. She wiped at the mirror enough to see her face and quickly twisted her hair into two large twists. Trey was humming in the shower. She decided to head downstairs to cook breakfast. Her headache was long forgotten.

Trey smiled as he washed. He'd be damn if his wife would be running around here calling any other man fine or cute. He'd have to make sure he put it on her more often. Damn how tired she claimed to be. It was true, over the years they had drifted apart. But the chemistry was always there. She could still make his toes curl. It was about time he started focusing on his wife and home. He did love her and the thought of losing her wasn't an option. The other women were a nice stroke to the ego, but none were worth more to him than Lex.

He'd have to cut it off with Tanya. He should have a long time ago. He never lingered long with any female. It was easier if he didn't give them enough time to develop any feelings. Though he always let them know upfront that he was a married man. More times than he could count these females began thinking that they could replace his wife. He tried a few times to let it go completely but then a cutie would catch his eye and the rest was history. He did make sure that he kept his relationships a secret and his rule was 3 months and on to the next. This didn't discourage some of these women from trying to hold on to him, but for many, surprisingly it was enough.

Lex never caught him, though she came damn close a few times. Even after Denise had approached her, he was able to construe enough doubt where she could never prove it. But this didn't stop her from playing detective. She used to spend a lot of time trying to catch him. She'd go through his phone. Login to his accounts, but he covered his tracks well. Besides, he never really talked with any of them. There wasn't any need to. It was strictly sex. He'd tried them hiding text apps, but it was all too much work for some pussy. He'd even resorted to paying some of them off to let it go. But as time went on, Lex quit trying to figure out what he was doing. She didn't ask where he was going or where he'd been anymore. He shaved and dressed while his thoughts wandered. The smell of bacon grease greeted him in the hall.

Now Lex could throw down in the kitchen. He

bounced to the music blasting from the kitchen. Lex and Lisa were in the kitchen dancing away to TLC. They'd had a mini concert after Lisa walked in behind Lex singing her heart out to a spatula and stepping it out. She came in on time, grabbed her mic (a wooden spoon), and joined in. After the song was over, they laughed until their stomachs hurt. Both Lisa and Lex could cook. Tye and Trey enjoyed their meals many nights at Lex's place. They used to have competitions to see whose dish was better.

They whipped up some grits, eggs, sausages, and biscuits. Lex reached into the fridge and grabbed a cantaloupe and quickly sliced up those and poured some orange juice into a pitcher. They were still dancing and singing while platting up the food. Lex glanced back at Lisa. "I miss you girl! We need to get together more often. We aren't even that far away from one another." "I know right.," Lisa responded. Trey walked in then. He laughed. "Awe hell no! I don't see my wife enough as it. But ya'll sure do got it smelling good up in here!" The doorbell rang and Lex looked at him with a raised eyebrow.

"Oh, that's just Rome. He's gonna go to the gym this morning with me." As he opened the door he turned back laughing "I finally convinced him to let me work with him some." Rome walked in smiling, "don't let him lie to you Lex. I'm being forced into this. A bet gone wrong," shaking his head he looked scared. "Lex, what you cooking girl? He rubbed his round belly, now this is more my speed. I know you got me a plate!" She chuckled. He had a permanent place at their table. "Come on in. We just finished up." Lisa waved at Rome, he wiggled his hips to the music and headed to the table. "Lisa my girl, how's it been?" They caught up as Trey whispered, "not sure if he's here for the food or Lisa. He was supposed to meet me at the gym until I mentioned Lisa was in town."

Rome has been crushing on Lisa since he first met her. Lisa kept him at arm's length for many years. When asked before why she would never give him a chance, she shrugged her shoulders and said that she wasn't into good boys. She might have a point because poor Rome would be wrapped around her finger. He followed her around like a puppy that entire weekend. All she had to say was I like this, and he would pull out his wallet. After a while she had to stop him, telling him boy keep your money in your pocket. I got my own money, before adding you're a sweetheart though. They were all settled at the table munching away when Lex asked, "Lisa you wanna hit the gym with the fellas?"

Trey looked up from his plate for the first time since he started eating. Lex hadn't been in the gym in a minute. "We could go in moral support of Rome", she laughed. Rome seemed to puff up his chest a little. "Don't let this round belly fool yall. Yo boy can lift some weights now. I can hold my own." "Alright, bet," said Trey. After eating Trey and Rome decided to head to the gym. The ladies would meet them there after getting dressed. In the car, Rome whistled "Ohhh weee. That damn Lisa is fine as hell. I don't know why she won't let a nigga holla at her."

"Boy, I told ya before, if you only knew, you'd stay clear of that one." Trey chuckled. "Man, I don't know why you ain't never hit that." Trey shook his head, "Man you crazy as hell. One, Lisa would beat my ass first then call Lex and the two of them would be digging my grave. Besides, I could never do that to Lex. Lisa is her girl." He may have stepped out a few times on Lex, but he would never mess with one of her friends. "Man, friends, homegirls, coworkers, anyone Lex may even know is off-limits." He did have some standards. He hadn't messed around as often as he made it seem like he did. Yea there were a few women, but before long he would lose interest. Sometimes he just needed some attention. Especially with Lex working so much and the kids. Man, them little cock blockers. He loved them but man did they put a damper on the fire that he and Lex had.

Lex and Lisa walked up into the gym and heads turned. "Damn, Lex, you ain't tell me Trey had stepped it up. The place looks great!" She shrugged, "what can I say, you know that this is his baby." There was a spin class going in one room, you could see them sweating it out. Everything was opened and each room was separated by soundproof glass. But you could see the entire space from the center desk. There was a spin room, aerobics room, separate rooms for weights and machines, and a racket ballroom. Besides, there was a dance studio, sauna, and massage parlor, which were Lex's added touch. On the other side, there was also a pool for water aerobics and swimming and a few jacuzzies to relax in after working out. Over the years Treachery had evolved. It attracted both the younger and older crowd. Lex had been thinking for a while about starting their own brand of health foods and drinks. Even clothing. This was next on her list. She may be able to use her nursing degree in their own business from the health and nutrition side. She mentioned this to Lisa as they walked through the building.

Trey spotted them walking through and waved them over. Rome was finishing a set. He was grunting and puffing but he quickly calmed down when he heard Lisa's voice. Damn, he was trying to get him to work on his breathing and to use that energy extra energy to center himself. His set was over, but he kept going. Trey reached under the bar and held it on his last lift. "That's enough bro. You don't want to overdo it." He gave the ladies a quick overview of the workout plan. Lex and Lisa stretched and warmed up then joined in. Trey would demonstrate first and then they all would complete a set together before moving on the next. Within minutes everyone was sweating and breathing heavily. They did a total body circuit. He missed working out with Lex. She could damn near keep up with him. Not to mention he loved looking at her. Her body was tight. It screamed strength but she could make certain areas jiggle when she wanted it to.

He smiled saying to himself "yea my baby fine". After working out they hit the showers and then headed out for lunch. They decided on a nice spot downtown near the strip. It was a beautiful day. The temperature was just right. As Lex reached for her glass of water, she looked up and met Brenden's gaze. He was sitting across from her a few tables down. She missed her glass spilling her drink. Yet, she still hadn't broken their eye contact. Lisa snapped her fingers "Lex". She blinked as she reached for a napkin. The cool water spreading across the table. She then took the napkin and dabbed it across her neck. Feeling flushed all of a sudden. Trey looked back in the direction that she had been looking.

"Hey babe, you ok." She stood suddenly.

"Yea, I might have overdone it today. It's been a while since I've worked out. I'm going to run to the restroom." Lisa stood but she waved her away. "I'm ok. Stay and chat it up with Rome she smiled." The restaurant was cool. She sighed in relief. It was a chic little mom-and-pop shop. The décor was light and airy. She headed to the back following the signs. Cute bamboo curtains separated the dining area. Behind the curtains were African American artwork and other trinkets for sale. The colors were bold, and each item was unique. She fingered a beautiful scarf before feeling someone behind her. They were too close to be a stranger. Thinking it was Trey she turned "Isn't this…she trailed off.

"Hey beautiful." She looked behind him, Trey was still at the table, his back to her.

She could see Lisa talking animatedly with her hands. Brenden cleared his throat. "Is that your husband" he smiled waving his hand as she did the night before. She smiled as well. He reached for her hand and she pulled back, attempting to turn away. He quickly tugged her into the hall that led to the restrooms. He pushed on the first door and pulled her inside. "What the f…." he placed his fingers across her lip. Letting his thumb linger on her lower lip. "Shhhh, she melted under his touch. He slowly backed her into a wall. "You cannot watch me with those bewitching eyes the way you were and not expect me to not want to touch you. You want me to touch you, don't you?" She inhaled shaking her head no. "You sure about that?" He lifted her hands above her head, holding them together with one hand. He reached down with his other hand skimming the side of her light summer dress. "You want me to stop?" She shook her head no. He reached under her dress and felt her lace underwear. "Hmmm, what color are these?" She whispered "green". He kissed her a soft, slow kiss that was left her lightheaded. As he kissed her, his fingers explored under her dress. She was trembling under his touch. Then suddenly he stopped. It was just what she needed to bring her back to her senses. "Omg, what were you thinking? What am I doing? I have to go." "Why? I know you enjoyed it. Hubby must not be doing his job. Your panties are soaked. What did you do with my number?"

She ignored his first statement. "I threw it out." He whispered the numbers in her ear. "Now repeat it." She stammers....9...8...6. He kneeled lifting her leg on his shoulder. He kissed the inside of her leg before she felt the cool tip against her skin. She reached down trying to stop him, but he quickly scribbled across her inner thigh. He stood.

"Commit it to memory and use it. I'll be waiting." With that, he walked out of the room. She glanced around as the door closed allowing just enough lighting for her to realize that they were in the powder room. She reached for the switch on the wall blinking as light flooded the room. She admired the cute little sitting area as she turned the knobs on the sink and splashed cool water on her neck and face, attempting to cool her heated skin.

Looking up in the mirror she was flushed. This was the first time she allowed another man to touch her. It was the first time another man had so much as turned her on. She stood staring at herself in the mirror. As she walked out of the restroom she almost collided with Lisa. "Lex, wtf!" I just saw Brenden. Did you see that fine mother fu…." Lex dragged her into the restroom. "Shut up!" "Oh, you did see him I take it." Lex looked away. "Shhh yes I saw him." Lisa smiled, her eyes sparkled.

"Ahh naaw…spill it!" "What you talking about?" "It's written all over your face. What did he say to you? I know you saw him. That's probably why your ass was taking so long." Lex shrugged her shoulders. "I don't know what you are talking about. Come on let's go before they start missing us." "Girl your ass has been missing. Why you think I came to get you. Trey was on his way in. But I told him I'd check on you. Good thing I did. You better tell him you got held up in the shop." "Oh, that reminds me. I did want that scarf!" They walked back through the shop together. But the scarf wasn't there. At the same time, the young girl behind the counter waved them over. She handed her a cute bag and inside was her scarf.

"That cute gentleman said it was for you. He described you to the t and I must admit you are as attractive as he said you were!" Lisa looked her up and down. "Umm hmmm. We most definitely talking about this later mam." They walked out laughing. Lunch was nice. They had a great time together. Lex had pushed Brenden to the back of her mind as they all caught up. Lisa appeared to be warming up to Rome.

As they headed home Trey reached for her hand and kissed it. It was something he used to do all the time. He looked over at her. "You know I love you, babe. I know I may not say it all the time, but I do." "Awww, Lisa yelled from the back seat. They laughed. "Trey old ass talking bout he still got swag!" "Shut up Lisa before

Rome grab your ass back there!" She glanced up in the rearview mirror and caught those two as they looked at one another. Lisa looked at her hand in her lap and Rome looked out the window.

Trey had this nagging feeling all week. He couldn't quite put his finger on it, but he hadn't left home much other than to work. They were back to their usual routine, but he felt a difference in Lex. Her response to him was different. Either that or he was tripping because it had been a while since he paid this much attention to her. He needed to slow his role. He had a good life. He had everything a man could ask for. Trey decided to pick up the kids today early. He'd surprise Lex at work and take them all out for dinner. His babies were excited to see him. After picking them up he headed over to the hospital.

He'd texted Lex and told her to meet him in the parking lot. She was surprised to see him but happy. She was tired and didn't feel like driving. She always kept a change of clothes in her locker to change out of her work clothes before going home. She used the laundry services at the hospital for her scrubs and jacket. They took the kids to Chucky Cheeses so that they could run around freely. Trey ran around with them, through the mazes, and played games while Lex relaxed and watched. She usually would run around too, but she was tired. It had been a crazy day at work. She thought back to the other day in the restaurant. The remnants of Brenden's number long gone from her skin.

However, his touch lingered. It was all she thought about it. Several days had passed and Trey was being the attentive husband and father. He didn't go out last weekend as he usually did but stayed at home. They watched movies together. First with the kids and then long after they had fallen asleep, they made love on the padded bed they'd made on the floor for the kids. They woke up the next morning in the same spot.

They were in a good place. Lex had the old Trey back. But it wasn't enough. Brenden had stirred something within her. She tried getting him out of her system by taking it out on Trey sexually. But it wasn't enough. Trey was enjoying it though and if she admitted it, she was too. However, Brenden had lit a fire within her that continued to smolder.

It was something about the way he watched her. He wanted her and had made it known. Sure, many men had approached her. But, for some reason. Brenden made her want him as well. She didn't forget his number, but she couldn't bring herself to dial it. Would she be so wrong to step out this once? How many times had Trey done it?

Damn Lex was wearing a nigga down. It had been years since she had put on a show and all. He loved to watch her dance for him. But between work, the kids, and the gym their sex life had become almost nonexistent. He missed the teasing and bantering they had in the bedroom and out. After a while, he used that as an excuse to see other women.

The ladies loved him, and his ring attracted them more. He wasn't getting the love and affection that he should be at home, so he sought it from other women. The sex was good. But that's all it ever was. He had his wife at home. He had everything he needed at home.

These hoes had some tricks that would have a nigga head spinning, but at the end of the night, he wanted to be home with his family, wrapped around his baby in their bed. He loved to hear the pitter-patter of feet early in the mornings. No one could replace Lex, and he'd bedded some bad bitches. But none compared to her beauty. She was the real deal. Not like these gold diggers who saw him as a paycheck.

Lex had her own and held him down many times when he was on the up and coming. He was thinking it was time to show her how much he appreciated her. Maybe upgrade her ring. Maybe even renew their vows. It was time for him to hang it up and recommit to his wife.

Her mentioning another man the other night was enough for him to start questioning how he would feel if she cheated on him. It wouldn't be pretty. He had to admit he'd probably be in jail. He thought about inviting her to dinner tonight. He was working on another project and might need her input.

Lex walked through the door. She expected Trey to be gone already but his car was still parked out front. She called his name as she walked through the house. "I'm upstairs", he yelled down. She was glad he had plans for the night. The kids were with their godparents for the weekend, and she planned on soaking in a hot tub of water until she pruned. She whistled when she saw Trey. "Damn my baby sexy. Boy, who you trying to impress?" "I told you I'm trying to seal this deal baby. He strutted across the room with a pimp walk. "I know I'm fine though." He threw her one of those knee-weakening smiles. "Why don't you get dressed and come with me tonight? We still have time." "Oh no you don't, I have a date with a hot oil bath and my pillow!"

"Ohh I love it when you talk dirty to me! He laughed. "Come on baby. I need you with me tonight. Come get a feel for these brothers and help your man close this! Please" he added. Besides, it's been a while since we got dressed up. "I guess. Give me a few minutes."

She went into the closet and pulled out a cute gold cocktail dress that he'd bought her a few months ago. She hadn't had a chance to wear it and it went well with his suit. She paired it up with some white and gold fuck me heels and laid it on the bed.

"Oh, hell yeah, my baby bout to mess up these boys head for real! He slapped her on the behind as she walked into the shower. She took a quick shower and twisted up her hair on one side, allowing her unruly curls to fall across the other side. She decided on light makeup but took a little more time with her eyes. The combination of her makeup and dress made her eyes pop. People always complimented her eyes. "Ohhh weee" Trey grabbed her from behind. He'd been watching her in the mirror applying her makeup. He dropped a kiss on her neck and lingered. "Maybe we need to cancel."

"You wanna dance for me again?" "Oh, no sir, not after I just got all cute." Her dressed hugged every inch of her stopping mid-thigh. Her legs went on for days and those shoes made him wanna beg. He kept trying to grab at her and she kept swatting his hands. "Come on now Trey before you start something!" He grabbed her again, "that is exactly what I'm trying to do! Fuck em". "Ah uh", she shoved him and grabbed her clutch. She walked off making her booty jiggle, she stopped at the door and looked back at him. "You coming?" She grinned. "I planned on all up in you, but you trippin."

Trey has been watching these brothers blow up online with their fitness classes and they developed a nice little following. He wanted to add them to his Treachery. He was explaining everything to Lex as they pulled up to the restaurant. It would be nice to add them to our lineup. He pulled up to the valet, one of the attendants opened the passenger door and assisted Lex out. He caught the appreciation in dude's eyes when he saw Lex. The young boy stuttered "evening mam." Trey walked up and placed his arms around her. "Thanks, young man."

Trey gave his name to the hostess and asked her to add another guest. She let him know that his other

guests were already seated and waiting for him. Lex
stumbled when Trey pulled out a chair for her at a table
that Bret and Brenden occupied. "What's up fellas. I
know I said it would just be me tonight, but this is my
wife, Alexia. "Good evening Alexia," Bret said. He
looked at Brenden his eyes widening. However, Brenden
didn't look surprised at all.

"Good evening Alexia." He said her name slowly
before sitting back in his chair. "I'm Brenden and this is
my brother Brent." Ok, she thought so they were going
to play this game. She cleared her throat. "Good
evening." Trey was next to her buzzing with
excitement. They ordered their drinks and then dinner.
After the waiter left Trey asked them what their plans
were. After listening to them he launched into a
discussion of expanding his online network. He wanted
to work with them and bring them under the Treachery
name. They would in turn receive stocks in the company
and an impressive salary. They would work in the main
gym and have their own space and creative freedom.
They would also launch a DVD series and online

website. Bret and Brenden liked the pitch. Especially when Trey told them their salary. Bret was all in, but Brenden hesitated. "Can we think it over and get back to you man?" Bret shot daggers at his brother. "What exactly are we waiting for?" Brenden was always the cautious one. "I'd like to have a lawyer look over the conditions first."

"Of course. I can understand that and recommend it" Trey responded. Lex was quiet most of the exchange. Trey had almost forgotten she was there. He squeezed her thigh. "I told you baby this was going to go good." They finished talking and decided to call it a night. "You guys have my number. Call me when you are ready to talk business." They all shook hands. Brenden held Lex's hand for a second longer willing her to meet his eyes. She looked away quickly mumbling "It was nice meeting you."

"Likewise," Brenden responded. Lex couldn't wait to call Lisa and fill her in on everything and it wasn't long before she ran into Brenden again. The next day she was off and stopped by the gym to take Trey lunch. She ran into Brenden in the hall. "Hello, Alexia. How are you doing.?" "I'm good Brenden. How about you?" "Much better now that I've seen you." She glared at him. "Don't." "Why not?" She looked up at him pleading with her eyes. "Please don't." "Fine, for now. I was just looking for Trey." "I'll show you to his office. I was just heading there." He followed her closely. "He's a lucky man," he said under her breath. She chose to ignore that comment. She walked into Trey's office and he quickly ended a call. He stood kissing her "Hey baby, I wasn't expecting you."

"I know, I was in the area and wanted to drop you off some lunch." "Mmm does part of my lunch include you?" Brenden cleared his throat behind her. It was the first time that Trey noticed that he was there. "Brenden! My man! What you got for me?" Lex used that time to escape. She kissed him on the cheek. "I'll see you later baby. Brenden, it was nice seeing you again." She left out of the room closing the door behind her.

This could not be good. This was not going to turn out good at all.

Lately, Brenden was turning up frequently. It's funny how she'd never seen this man a day in her life before she went out with Lisa. Now she seemed to be running into him everywhere. She was shopping on the other side of town and decided to check out a massage parlor she passed in the shopping center. She liked to check her competition and see what the other places were offering. She was at the counter checking in for a massage. She'd checked online ahead of time, and they had an opening, so she signed up.

Somehow, there was a mix-up in the schedule, and they did not have any rooms available. As she turned to leave, Brenden walked up behind her. "I couldn't help but overhear what happened. Why don't you join me? I have a reservation for a couple's massage. She looked around him. "A couple's massage usually includes two people." "Well, it was the only one available, so I booked it. I've already paid for two people so you might as well join me." "I'll pass. But thanks." "Come on it isn't like we'll be alone. If you don't trust me" he smiled mischievously.

She muttered, "it's me that I don't trust around you." "What was that?" he asked. He smiled at the receptionist. Mrs. Alexia will be joining me today." He winked at Lex "I promise to keep it PG."

Lex gave in and trailed behind the receptionist and Brenden. She admired him from behind as he walked ahead of her. In the room, robes hung on the door. She refused to get undressed in front of him. That was taking it a bit too far. She asked if they could have separate rooms. "I'm sorry but we don't have any extra rooms, but we do have partitions that could divide the room if you'd like. "Oh, that sounds great" she answered quickly. Brenden chuckled but didn't say anything in response. Now she could relax and enjoy her massage.

They started her off with a hot stone massage. She lounged on her stomach as the masseuse placed the warm stone across her back. While she worked a vibrating rhythm from her shoulders down. She heard a moan from behind the divider. His grunts and moans becoming louder. You'd think she was doing more than just massaging him. She asked for headphones turning the relaxing music up.

The massage felt so good. She dozed off for a few minutes. She woke to deeper pressure on her lower back and moaned in pleasure. They must have switched because this person was hands were rough. She hadn't asked for a deep tissue massage, but it felt great. The hands massaged her lower back, her hips, buttocks, and thighs.

She groaned again enjoying the feeling. It was then that the masseuse leaned over her removing one of her earbuds. "I knew you'd enjoy my touch much more." She froze at the sound of Brenden's voice. "What the hell do you think you are doing?" She started to sit up, then realizing her position she laid back down. "Don't worry they won't be back for another 15 minutes. I made sure of it." "Get out Brenden!" "I would if you wanted me to. But you don't want me to do you? I won't touch again until you ask. But I promise that you will be begging for my touch one day soon."

"Come on Brenden. I already told you that I am married. Yes, I am attracted to you ok. Does that make you feel better? But that is all. I'm just attracted to you. It's a natural feeling. You're a good-looking man." He smiled. "But I will never act on it. So, get over yourself."

"Too late." "Too late for what?" "If that were all you wouldn't have been moaning my name as a massaged you. It was not your husband's name that you called. It was mine. You might as well let me scratch that itch for you." She placed her hand on her forehead groaning out loud.

"We have 10 minutes left. I could do so much in 10 minutes. It would be the best 10 minutes of your life." Though she wanted to, she couldn't bring herself to do it. Why was it so easy for men to cheat? As if reading her mind, he said "We both are adults. It's perfectly natural to be attracted to someone other than your husband. What you don't know is that I am married as well." "Was that supposed to make me feel better?

Knowing that you are married. I could never make another woman feel that pain." She stopped suddenly already saying too much.

"So, he has cheated on you? I can tell by your response. So now what's really stopping you? Your body is begging to be touched. I can take that pain away that I see in your eyes." She couldn't believe she was considering it. She licked her lips. "I could do that for you too," he said and staring at her mouth. She wanted to go for it. She wanted Trey to feel the pain she felt. She wanted for once to throw all caution in the wind and not have to always be the bigger person. To not be the one that always had to make the responsible choice. For once she wanted to not be in control. Not worry about consequences. "If I agree, it has to be only one time. No strings attached. And you cannot take the job at the gym." She thought for sure that he would choose the job, but he answered quickly. "When and where? He moved as quickly as he answered. I'm many things, but I'm not a 5-minute brother. Besides, I'm going to need much more time...." "Not here of course." "I could arrange…" "No, it will be under my terms. The when, the where." "Let me give you a sneak preview". He leaned close to her. She waited for him to kiss her closing her eyes. But nothing happened. He was watching her. "I promised that I wouldn't touch you again until you asked me." She couldn't believe she was doing this. "Ok fine, kiss me." "That wasn't a question, that was demand. Try again." She was becoming frustrated. "Kiss me please." "Kiss me please who?" Somehow, he was even closer to her. Her skin tingled from the nearness of him. "Kiss me please, Brenden." "I thought you'd never ask. I also want to know that you know exactly who you are kissing." He leaned forward and time and space stopped. He deepened the kiss and she sat up trying to get closer to him.

Her towel fell from her breast and he groaned deep. He quickly ducked his head and pulled a nipple into his mouth. She moaned out loud. She heard footsteps approaching. She tried to pull away, but he reached his arm around him pulling her closer. "Brenden stop. Please!" In her mind, she was screaming please don't stop. But the footsteps came nearer stopping at the door. There was a light knock on the door signaling her return.

He dropped a quick kiss on her lips. "Preview" he reminded her. She hurriedly pulled the towel back across her and returned to her stomach. It was silent on the other side of the curtain. "What was he, part damn cat?" she thought. She thought about sleeping with Brenden. She had admitted that she wanted him, but that was all it was going to be. It was an internal battle she fought daily. How the hell did men cheat and not feel guilty or apprehension? She loved Trey with everything in her. But she had given him everything and what did she get in return? It wasn't as if it had happened once, no he had to keep hurting her over and over again. Brenden was never far from her mind. She kept picturing that smile. It didn't help that he was so good-looking. He stood about 5 ft 10. He was just so damn sexy, and he wanted her. He made it known in every encounter. She could still feel his lips, his touch. Every time she thought of him and their brief encounters her body heated up.

She knew that he was going to be addicting. It was as if once he touched her, her body craved more. It had been weeks since the couple's massage. She was in bed alone as usual. Trey was downstairs in his man cave doing whatever it is that he found to do there every night. She'd just finished washing her vibrator and placed it carefully back into his satin bag. Brenden had started a thirst that Trey nor "Trill" that was what she'd nicknamed her purple 10 pulsations remote-operated egg, could quench. She had to slow down in the bedroom with Trey after she was so lost in her fantasy of Brenden that his name almost fell from her lips at the height of her release. When she'd opened her eyes, she felt disappointed that it wasn't him. Lex was always a firm believer of the saying "do unto others as you would have them do unto you". But she was also one of those kids that lived in the now and would take a good ass whooping later if she felt that it was for a good cause. That sense of rebellion was building up in her again. She'd saved his number in her phone under Tiffany.

She didn't know who the hell Tiffany was but, she and Brenden had developed a healthy sexting relationship. Over a few weeks, she had indulged him in every bedroom desire that she had ever had. He asked and she'd told him all her secrets.

What turned her on. How hard, fast, even if she preferred short or long strokes. Most of these were answers to questions that he had asked. He in return gave her detailed examples of how he could and would please her. His attention to detail in his words painted such a vivid picture that it could have been a short film she watched in her mind. If he could pay that much attention to details in words, she could only imagine how he could to her body.

Whenever Trey was asleep or off entertaining whatever flavor of the week, he'd picked up at the gym. She would retreat to her study and message Brenden. She'd long ago stop caring because it wasn't as if Trey was stopping. For a long time, she wondered how she became one of those wives that endured the other women and lies. She tortured herself in her web of psychological abuse trying to understand why he did what he did. She spent years trying to compete, to be someone that she wasn't, to look younger, fitter. She tried to be the perfect wife and mother. She'd even resorted to all-out begging him to stop, threatening to kill herself, threatening to kill him. Still, he never stopped maybe for a few months, but it wouldn't be long before he started stepping out of the room to take a call or sitting in his car on the phone for long periods. Coming home late, showering immediately, and then crawling into bed claiming that he was exhausted from work.

Brenden was very convincing, and it wasn't long before she agreed to see him. She registered for an upcoming conference. She put in for vacation and had two weeks off immediately after the conference. That meant that she had a total of three weeks off consecutively. Something that she had not had in years. In fact, she hadn't used more than a few days of her vacation in years. This way she could spend a week with Brenden. Return home and take a vacation with her family and then have a week to rest before returning to work. The closer her time off neared the more nervous she became. Trey was going to know something was up because she was so nervous.

Trey was becoming annoyed with everything and everyone. He realized that he was no longer enjoying his playboy lifestyle. He wasn't sure if he was just growing tired of it all or if it was because Lex seemed to be doing her own thing lately. She barely looked his way. Didn't complain or ask where he'd been. The few minutes of pleasure he was getting outside of his home was no longer pleasuring.

The thrill was gone. He could get that at home. Lex was spending more and more time locked away in her study. She was taking more online courses and said that she was studying, but damn it ain't that much studying in the world. The thing was, the tired worn-out lines were gone from her face. She smiled more, though not with him. He found himself watching her more. Wanting to spend more time with her, but she didn't have time for him. It was work, school, the kids as usual.

He used to love the distractions because that meant she would be nagging him less. But now he wanted her attention. He tried offering to take a jog with her in the evenings, massage her feet, take her out for dinner and she seemed to enjoy it all. But he felt something else was missing. It was her fault. His insecurities were blocking his game. Either that or he was just getting older, and the thrill was gone.

Day one of vacation was officially here. She had an early flight out to Miami. Her entire weekend was planned out and she was more than ready. It was almost as fun as planning her honeymoon. It was well deserved, and she was going all out. It was about time someone enjoyed all the effort she put into looking as good as she did. She had rented a beachfront condo equipped with a jacuzzi, private beach access, jet skis, and more. The rooms and estate were gorgeous in the online photos. She didn't even feel as guilty as she thought she would. It was finally her time to live, to indulge, and do what the hell she wanted to do. There was a little apprehension, but her excitement overrode it. She had never been with

another man. Trey was her first and only. She had
learned everything there was to know about sexual
intimacy from him, books, videos, and her girls. She
didn't have any sisters and well it wasn't
something she could ever ask her brother. She wondered
if Brenden would enjoy being with her. He seemed to
know his way well around a woman's body and mind.
She was riding first class. She was lounging in the
compact bed. Yes, she did say bed.

She was pleasantly surprised when she arrived at
the airport and was told that her coach ticket had been
upgraded to first class. She also received a bottle of wine
with a note from Brenden *to enjoy yet another preview of what
being with me entails, Brenden.* From her arrival at the
airport to being led to her small suite would be an
unforgettable experience. The terminal was unlike any
she'd ever seen. Furnished with comfortable armchairs
and sofas. There was a private separate bar with a drink
option that put the usual watered-down drinks in
airports to shame. The digital system was larger than the
usual headrest sets in coach with an endless library of

entertainment. She was served a 5-star, full course meal to include the white linen tablecloth and fine china. She was enjoying the pampering. The suite was carpeted with plush toe-curling carpet. She had immediately removed her shoes to sink her toes in it. There was also a personal shower and closet for her luggage. She didn't have to check any bags or fight for overhead space. She was lying back when she heard the familiar ring of the bell and the deep baritone voice of the captain announced that they would be landing soon. Deplaning was swift and even this was done in style.

There was a car waiting for her to include a driver who stood in the lobby holding up a gold and black sign with her name. She was beginning to feel like a star. She was taken to her beautiful beachfront home away from home. From the gateway to the door the landscaping was gorgeous. In the distance, she could see the beautiful blue sea sparkling.

The home was impressive. She strolled up the walkway following the driver who placed her luggage at the door and tipping his hat. "Good day mam." Her heart skipped a beat. She couldn't believe she was here and what was about to take place. She stood at the doorway for a few moments, letting it all sink in. She still had time to turn back and count her blessings. Just as she turned to wave to the driver the door opened. Brenden leaned on the doorframe and leaving was forgotten.

"Hey, beautiful." She cleared her throat smiling in return, "hi." He stood there watching her intently. They stood this way for several minutes just staring at one another. "Are you planning on coming in? I promise I don't bite." She wouldn't mind if he did, she thought to herself. It was something about this man that made her knees weaken. She stepped forward as he stepped back allowing her to pass. He reached out wheeling her luggage into the foyer and shut the door. The sound echoed in her ears. She stood; her feet felt rooted to the floor. She looked up at him wondering what he was thinking, but his face gave away nothing. He was relaxed except for the occasional pulsing she noted at his temple.

"I wasn't sure you'd show. You look like you're ready to run." She looked down and he asked with his head tilted. "Why did you come?" "Because I wanted to. I want this" she said waving her hands in his direction. It was not right for someone to be this fine.

Just the sound of his voice made her come undone. "Come here," he said when her eyes made it back up to his. She didn't move so he moved closer to her. "Can I at least get a hug?" he asked. She needed to get this over with. Get this, him out of her system. This was her real reason for coming here. She said so out loud. He waited for her to make the next move. She placed her hands on his chest. Needing to touch him. She moved her hands down to his waist unzipping his pants. He continued watching her. He was naked beneath it. "Look at me" he commanded. His skin was smooth, thick veins running across him. He leaned down and kissed her. He hardened more as he did. She tried pulling her hand away, but he gripped it around him. With his other hand, he placed a light pressure on the back of her neck, then slowly made circles sending chills up her spine. It was one of her erogenous zones. He remembered. He moved her hand up and down his length before groaning and lifting her.

He walked until her back touched the wall. She wrapped her legs around him as he trailed kisses across her exposed shoulders and chest. Her head fell backward giving him more access. She had worn a strapless dress and had decided to ditch her underwear at the last minute. He reached under her dress and smiled, dipping one of his thick fingers within her. She was slowly coming apart. He placed another finger then a third stretching her. He moved slowly leaving her trembling.

"You like this, he asks?" She nodded her head. "Let me hear you say it." "Yes…. mhhh yes I do." "Is this all you wanted?" She shakes her head. "Tell me you want more." She moaned loudly "I want more." There labored breathing loud in her ears. Their lovemaking was quick and rough. Still clothed up against the wall. He seemed to touch every inch of her and spoke roughly to her. She wasn't used to being so verbal during sex. It was as if he needed confirmation of everything she felt.

He kept asking as he stroked her "How do you like that? Tell me how that feels to you. Do you want more?" She answered enthusiastically wanted to please
him. It ended as suddenly as it began. But she was thoroughly satisfied. She slid down him until her feet touched the floor. Their skins damp. Their breathing erratic. She laid her head on his chest trying to regain her composure.

He laughed. "Let me show you the rest of the house. He took her by the hand and lead her down the hall and up a set of winding stairs. They move through the house silently; she was enjoying the view of him from behind. He walked her into the master suite passing a huge king-sized poster bed. He led her into the bathroom where he undressed her slowly exploring her body as he went. He reached behind her turning on the shower. He undressed quickly and stepped into the shower and pulling her in behind him.

Everything about this day had been unbelievable. Everything was beyond beautiful. She wondered if she would wake from this dream. It had been a long time since Trey had spent so much time pleasing, encouraging, or praising her. It was the first time she thought of him. The contrast between the two men was night and day. Where Trey was dark and had a slightly larger build; Brenden's tone was lighter, his skin smoother. Brenden was also taller, his hair curly. Both men were generous beneath the waist, though even that was different. Brenden was a more generous lover.

"Keep watching me like that and I won't be responsible for my actions." She had been lost in her comparisons and she hadn't realized that he was watching her. He took a sponge and washes her from head to toe. Slowly, meticulously lingering on areas that he knew turned her on.

She climaxed again just from his touches. It had been a long time since she had been this responsive. It was equally as long since she'd felt this level of lust and need. The way he watched her made her feel wanton, desired, and beautiful. She continued the rest of the evening on a high.

He brought her things upstairs and they lounged in bed for the rest of the evening. They talked most of the night sharing intimate things about themselves. She had texted Trey and her mother letting them know that she had arrived and then he had her turn her phone off and hand it to him. They had agreed that for 24 hours she would be all his and he spent the rest of the night trying to erase any thoughts of home. He was very good at doing so. She experienced the kind of lovemaking that had her climbing the sheets and trembling and pulsating long after it was over.

She woke the next morning disoriented. But it all came to her in pieces. It was all real. She was here with Brenden and she'd allowed him to do things to her body that even her husband had never done. She pushed away any feelings of guilt or shame and kept telling herself that she deserved this. All she had to do was remind herself of how many times that Trey had done this to her. Then, would return to her sometimes with another woman's scent still on his skin. She had told Brenden what she wanted, and he fulfilled it all and more. Why should she feel guilty? They had promised one another a weekend. No strings attached guilt-free. This weekend they could be whoever they wanted and just enjoy their piece of paradise.

It was just that. Everything was private. They had a private beach and pool. Brenden branded toe-curling memories in both. The home was stocked with food. He was great with making her forget everything. It was easier because she was not herself there. She didn't know who this nymphomaniac was that was here with Brenden. A condition of her coming to him was that he wouldn't take the job with Treachery. He could have her all to himself to do whatever he pleased and then they would never see each other again.

They walked the grounds holding hands. They went jet-skiing, snorkeling, and swam in the ocean. Evenings were spent feeding each other, she'd never look at food the same. They took advantage of every minute. But the end of their time together was drawing near. Trey and home were a distant memory that she knew she would have to soon face.

She forwarded all his calls and sent him short texts, telling him that her days were long and that she was physically and mentally drained by the end of the day. At least there was some truth in that. It was easier to be dishonest in text than verbally. She did have brief conversations with her mom and the kids. She would fill their few minutes with dozens of questions, not leaving time for them to ask her any. She found it more difficult to be dishonest with them. He'd give her space, but if she spent too long, he would distract her in a way that had her rushing to end their call. She wasn't sure if he spent that time calling home himself.

On the last evening, Brenden told her that they were going out to a party. It was formal and he had purchased her a gorgeous gown to wear. It was the first sign of unease since they had arrived. She reminded him that they had agreed to stay in the condo or private property. But he reassured her that the party was private as well, and only vacationers were there, and they were in the off-season so it would probably be only a few others. "Trust me he added." He told her that he had wanted to see her all dolled up as she was at the restaurant with Trey. It was the first time he mentioned her husband. He shared with her how he fantasized about doing much of what he had this weekend to her on the table that they sat at. She was impressed with his style. The dress was classy yet teasing. She spent a deal of time with her hair and makeup.

She peeped in the mirror and was satisfied. She emanated bad bitch. Guess she was her own Sasha fierce tonight. When she walked down the stairs Brenden gawked. "You clean up nice." "You do as well", she replied. He took her hand, twirled her around, and dipped her back. "You are gorgeous. Not only physically but everything about you. I enjoyed this weekend with you." "The feelings mutual." "Thank you for trusting me," he paused as if he wanted to say more. "I just want you to know I could love you and show you just how much you are worth." She smiled in return.

"You've done a great job showing that and more." He led her out the door and she asked where was the car? He told her that it wasn't far, and he'd rather walk. He led the way and she followed. "Have you been here before?" she asked. "No, but I did arrive a few hours before you and received a tour, that's how I found out about the party." "Oh, ok."

The event was just as promising and glamourous as her entire experience. The food was amazing. The music was seductive as was the tone of the evening. Brenden's dancing was just as intoxicating as his lovemaking. Everything about this man was addicting.

Soon after Lex left, Tanya hit Trey up asking if he wanted to join her for the weekend. He declined initially, then decided Lex was out doing her nursing thing so why not? She was miles away and the kids were gone for the weekend as well. He hadn't heard from Tanya in a while.

It had been months, but she had a way of leaving a man wanting more. She told him that she had a beach house for the weekend and that her friends had all bailed out. It wouldn't be fair for her to go all alone. She promised to make it worth his while and they never had to leave the bedroom. He packed a bag and was on the next flight. Tanya looked great as usual. She was a little thicker, but it looked good on her. He couldn't wait to part them thighs.

The thin material that hugged her hips had his mouth-watering. He spent most of their time together learning and exploring every new curve. He was leaving in the morning and decided that he would end things with Tanya for good.

He enjoyed her, but he realized she was getting attached and a little too comfortable. There was something off with her this time as well. He couldn't put his finger on it, but she was beginning to make him weary. He reminded her that he had a wife at home and that impromptu trips such as this was a good way to get caught. She waved him off saying she knew he had a wife. He didn't have to keep reminding her. She had a husband as well. He was surprised because this was the first time that he had heard of this. He asked her where her husband was, and she responded with a shrug of her shoulders. If she had wanted to know where he was or think about him, she would have brought him along, she told Trey.

Trey had his hands on her hips as she swayed to the music. This place was like no other and he'd been to some nice spots all over the world. He was enjoying how she felt against him. He was going to miss their spontaneous get-togethers. She grinded up against him making him ready to remove the layer of clothing between them.

She began stroking him on the dancefloor. She tried undoing his pants. He pulled her close "Damn girl. You gonna rape a nigga on the dance floor?" This made her grind against him even more. He groaned "let's go…now" pulling her behind him. She laughed "Come on we can do it right here." He pulled her further away from the party. They walked from under the lights strung up above them, leaving the music and crowd behind them. He sought a private area. Only a few people strolled past them. Damn, Tanya had maybe a few drinks, but it wasn't enough to have her acting like this.

He wondered if someone slipped her something or if she'd had more than just a drink. He didn't think she was into drugs or anything. Tanya ducked into a corner that was hidden from view. She dropped to her knees pulling at his pants. "I want to taste you now." She was always wild, but he'd never seen her like this. "Relax baby," she said as she released him from his pants. Once she got started Trey forgot about where he was and let her take control. He was lowkey turned on more by her public display. She stood after several minutes, turned around lifting her dress, and swatted her ass. She laughed out loud. He gave her what she was asking her for, driving in and out of her from behind. Her soft moans grew louder and louder.

Brenden swayed to the music with Lex. He watched Trey and Tanya from a distance. He pulled Lex closer with her back to them and kept his head turned in her neck. He was surprised Tanya wasn't alone. He had rented her a private condo as well, but it was supposed to be for her alone. Trey being there was a bonus. Maybe he wouldn't have to send him the videos of him and

Tanya after all. He watched as they headed towards the beach. He invited Lex to take a stroll with him along the beach. She followed unaware of the events unfolding. He walked her to a bench removing her shoes and offering a foot rub. He'd watch the two dip into the shadows and was waiting for them to step out. The dim lights that lined the walkways created shadows in the dark. She was enjoying his foot rub with her eyes closed. She mumbled thank you to him.

He heard a faint moan from the direction that Tanya and Trey were. After a few more moans he was sure it was Tanya. Lex sat up looking wide-eyed at him, "is that?" He brought one finger to his mouth whispering "shhh." He motioned for her to stand. Though he knew it would hurt seeing them together, he needed her to see them. He fought to keep calm. "Wanna have some fun?"

"Leave them people alone and let them have some privacy", she whispered giggling. But he was already tugging her in that direction. A new sense of urgency took over. They quietly followed the sounds of passion. "Have you ever watched someone make love" he asked quietly? "Not like on television but live?" He thought about the time Tanya convinced him to have a threesome and had him watch her with another man. She had in turn returned the favor by bringing another woman into their bed as well. Lex shook her head no. "It's different", he paused. "But arousing." "I don't know about that, but ok, if you say so." He looked at her once more. Feeling slightly sorry for doing this to her. But he couldn't stop himself if he wanted to. He pulled her into the shadows on the other side of the couple oblivious to their new audience.

Lex couldn't believe what they were doing. Brenden held her close and they watched together. This wasn't her thing, so after a few minutes, she turned away. Brenden never looked away and he was rigid. His hands clenched at his side. "Tell me what you see?" His voice was cold. A shiver ran up her spine. She stood in front of him trying to divert his attention. "Brenden, I don't like this", she said touching his face. He continued to stare for a few seconds longer then looked down at her.

"Lex, I'm sorry. I thought that this would be easier." He looked broken. "Turn around and look again." "No, I don't want to. Let's just go. I'm starting to feel like some sick peeping Tom." Brenden still had not moved. "Fine you stay" she began to walk away. Thinking to herself, I knew it was all too good to be true. What was she thinking? She didn't know enough about Brenden to have gone for a weekend alone with him. As she turned, she heard a familiar voice. She froze. Turning to Brenden she asked, "What did you just say?" She was shaken because for a second, he sounded like Trey. She thought to herself that the weekend was catching up to her and she must be tired. But this time she heard his voice again and she was looking at Brenden. She turned towards the couple. The guy was pulling up his pants as the woman straightened her dress.

"Damn baby, I feel like a new man." Maybe she was hallucinating. Because this man sure did sound, and now that she thought about it stood like her husband. She walked towards them. He embraced the woman and they began walking towards her. As they neared each other she said "Trey?" He stopped walking dropping the woman's shoes. He looked like he'd seen a ghost. "Lex?" Brenden came behind her. "Great so everyone knows everyone I see. Except maybe you two, he says nodding towards Lex and the other woman. "Tanya, I see you still enjoy being fucked in compromising positions."

Lex pulled from him heading full speed towards Trey. Brenden reached her just as she lunged for him. "Brenden? Yo man, I don't know what kind of fucking games you're playing but get your hands off my wife." "Funny how you are suddenly thinking of your wife after we just watched you fucking *my* wife. How was it by the way? No comparison in my opinion to Lex here." Lex elbowed him in his gut, cutting off his rant.

Trey walked in her direction "Babe?" "No, no, no" she looked back and forth between the three of them. "You better not even think of coming near me Trey." "I mean it." "Listen, Lex…" "You too Brenden…. just shut the fuck up" she shouted! "Naw, I'm done shutting the fuck up. I've watched these two sneak around not caring that they both had a spouse at home." He spat. "Do you know how many nights I waited at home, you waited at home while these two were together?! You carried his son and made me think he was ours! His voice broke. I hoped and prayed he was mine, but he looks just like this mother fucker" he motioned towards Trey.

"What?!" Lex turned to Trey. Her voice was cold. "What baby Trey?" Her head bobbing between Trey and Tanya. "What fucking baby?" Trey stood looking back and forth between Brenden and Lex, rubbing his beard. It was as if he hadn't heard anything Brenden said. "I thought you were away at a conference. So, was he at the conference too?"

"Oh, you just now getting it?" Brenden asks. How does it feel to know someone else been screwing your wife? I spent all weekend exploring all of her" he smiled. "I'm still trying to figure out what baby Trey" Lex shouted! "You telling me you slept with my wife?" Trey walked towards Brenden. "Lex? I asked you a mother fucking question, Lex." His voice was deadly.

For the first time, Tanya speaks, and her voice stops everyone. Her voice was still. Void of emotion. She looks at Trey. "Our baby. I was going to tell you tonight Trey. I knew you'd leave her once you found out about him."

"Oh no…and this bitch crazy? All ya'll mother fuckers crazy," Lex throws her hands up. She turns to Brenden. "Brenden. Thanks…." she turns towards Trey and stares him dead in the eyes "for an amazing weekend. That was up until now. Yall two can deal with crazy ass over there," she tosses up her hands. She was tired. Sick and damn tired and she was pissed that they had spoiled her perfect weekend. She walked away leaving the three of them behind her. She'd sleep in the airport if she had to, but there was no way she was going back with Brenden or Trey.

A week passed, and Lex finally decided that it was time to go home. She ran back to the condo, grabbed her things, and called a ride. Instead of going home, she stayed at a hotel. It was there that she found that she could catch a boat to the Keys. The only person that she called was Lisa and filled her in on the details of her weekend from start to finish. She ended up turning off her phone after she received numerous calls from Trey and Brenden. She refused to answer any other of them. She asked Lisa to call her mom. She didn't have the energy to talk with her. Lisa would know what to tell her. She wasn't sure why she'd gone to the Keys. All she knew was that she needed an escape. She spent the entire week in her room. She spent the first few days in silence, finally venturing out. She flirted with a few of the guys at the bar. Drank herself sick and slept with a different man every night thereafter. A wounded female must have emanated from her because every guy approached her asking "What's wrong…Are you ok…." or her favorite "I can erase any and everything you're feeling right now."

She tried to erase how good Brenden made her feel and Trey altogether. But either Brenden had spoiled it for every other man, or the alcohol had. The more she rebelled the sicker she felt. Physically and emotionally. She had never thought past sleeping with Brenden. She had never expected Trey to find out. It was supposed to be her little victory. Somehow, she thought that it would replace the hurt and shame she felt when she thought of him with another woman.

The flight home was short. She arrived in Atlanta late. The house was dark, and Trey's car wasn't home. She opened the door and walked through the house turning on the lights as she entered each room. She thought she'd feel different being back home. But the truth of the matter was she felt indifferent. She was glad that Trey wasn't there. She wasn't ready for the conversation that they were going to have to have. She didn't even know where to begin. Trey had the nerve to look hurt when he saw her with Brenden. She had been foolish to have fallen for Brenden. She turned on the shower and walked back into the room undressing as she went. She just wanted a hot shower and to sleep in her own bed, alone tonight.

She was grabbing her nightclothes when a sound made her pause. She thought she had heard someone. She peeked out the window. Trey's car was still not outside. She reached into her drawer and opened the black case and loaded her small pink 9 mm Glock. Trey had made sure that she could protect herself and had insisted that she take a concealed weapons class and purchase a firearm. She walked in the direction that she heard the sound. She heard the voice again. It sounded like someone was singing. She felt a chill run up her spine. The female voice was familiar. She walked into the guest room slowly. Her gun held out in front of her. She turned on the light and found Tanya rocking back and forth in a rocking chair. "What the fu…," she stopped and looked around the room with her gun steady on Tanya. A new crib and rocker were in the room. Her eyes circled back to Tanya who was rocking back and forth. She held a small bundle wrapped in a blanket.

"Shhhh," she said, or you'll wake the baby, and you may want to put that away, she motioned towards the gun. "It's about time you showed up. We've been waiting for you. Me and our son that is." She smiled, "He does look like Trey. Would you like to meet your stepson? Here you can hold him." She stood handing

Lex the baby. Lex reached for him. It was more of a reflex as Tanya dropped him in her arms. Lex felt like she had entered the twilight zone. The bundle of blankets was light. She placed the gun in her waistband and pulled back the blanket. She was surprised to see a small baby. He was really small and emaciated. Tanya had sat back down and began singing rocking again. Lex thought that the baby was dead until she saw him move slightly. Tanya was having a full conversation with herself. Her words moving as fast as the rocker.

"We've been here for three days now. Yall didn't have any baby milk here…I've been breastfeeding though. But I think my supply is just about gone, plus I don't think he likes my milk at all. He doesn't seem to like me. Cries all the damn time for his daddy. You know that little mother fucker told me he would rather live in this nice big ass house with his dad and you. Hell, I told him we all gonna live here." Lex faintly registered what she was saying. She left Tanya and rushed down the hall. She ran to her room and throwing a robe around her and quickly placed the gun back in the case. She thought about it and locked it. Taking the key with her. Tanya's voice raised as Lex ran downstairs. She wasn't sure what she was talking about now. She grabbed her phone dialing the ER as she ran from the house.

Hi. This is Alexia, RN. I'm the floor manager of mother-baby. Can I talk to the pediatrician right now? Her voice was much calmer than what she felt on the inside. Her heartbeat and thoughts running a race. How the hell did she get into my home? Where in the hell is Trey? "Look it's in an emergency. If a pediatrician is not near give me an attending."

"Hi, Lex" it's me, Jasmine. We've worked a few shifts together. I'm one of the float nurses…" "Hey, Jazz, again this is an emergency. I need to talk to the doc now" she yelled. She was already driving. "Sure, Dr. Brayburn is right here actually." Lex started talking not waiting to hear the doctor say hello. "Dr. Bray.
It's Lex. Hey, I have a newborn baby here. He doesn't look good. He's tiny, weak, and very malnourished. His breathing is very shallow. I…. I just found him. I don't know if he's going to make it. I think it was quicker for

me to get to the hospital than wait on EMS to make it to me.

I can't go into detail but have a team ready. I don't know how many months he is…. He can't be more than a few pounds. I'm really surprised he's alive!" She drove erratically to the hospital with the baby in her arms. I'm only a few minutes out. You're gonna need the pediatric code team. She kept glancing down at the baby. He was curled into the fetal position. She would stir him slightly and be relieved each time he moved. Her heart ached for the baby in her arms.

He reminded her of the small kitten she brought home when she was a kid. She turned another corner, the hospital signs coming into view. Her thoughts cleared as she heard Dr. Brayburn shouting out orders. She hadn't realized she was still on the phone. "Lex, you should have called EMS. How far are you?" "I'm pulling in now." She pulled up to the ER entrance, barely getting the gear into the park before running out. Dr. Brayburn was standing in the doorway. She handed for the baby and Lex ran behind her down the corridor.

Dr. Brayburn was speaking fast but calmly. Lex ran with her grabbing things and she headed to the pediatric trauma room. "Lex you're not dressed or even on the clock." "Is this your baby?" "Mines…no." She gave Dr. Brayburn a bewildered look.

"Go up to your office and wait on me. Call the police. You need to give them a report and call social services. I'll let you know when he is out of the woods. Don't leave!" She whispered as the nurses closed the doors. Lex stood outside the door, her adrenaline pumping. She should be in there too. What the hell had Trey and Brenden gotten her into? Where the hell were they? She called Trey first, his phone going to voicemail. She then called Brenden. He answered immediately. "Lex, is that you? I am so sorry." "Save it. Do you know where your wife is?" "Let me explain." "I take it that you don't since I just left her crazy ass in my home." "Your home? What are you talking about Lex?" "Tanya? That is her name, right? Yea, that nut job was sitting in my house with her baby."

"Baby, Lex wait, slow down. Tanya? You've seen her? She ran out of the house with the baby a few days ago. I don't think she is well Lex. She returned the next day without the baby. Swearing that she had given him up for adoption. She had the paperwork and all. I've been looking for her. She left talking crazy. Saying how she was moving in with you guys and that you were helping with the baby. I have been trying to reach you and Trey."

"I don't know Brenden, but ya'll are freaking me out. She was at the house with the baby alone. I don't know how she even got into my house. I just got home maybe an hour ago. I haven't talked to Trey since I left you all at the beach." She paused. Her heart dropping. "Oh my God. What if she has done something to Trey, Brenden? I'm at Mercy Hospital. You need to get here now. The baby, I don't know if he's going to make it. I can't right now. I need to call the police and find Trey." She hung up dialing 911. "Hello, this is Alexia Stewart. My address is…" she rambled off. I need an officer to check my home. I found a woman…." she stuttered "an intruder in my home." "No, I am not home. I am at the hospital." "No, I am not hurt. But I think that my husband might be. By the woman."

"Did the woman hurt your husband?" "I don't know, mam could you please just dispatch an officer to my home? The woman may be dangerous, or I don't know if dangerous but in danger." Damnit, she did not want anyone to be a casualty of the police. "Mam she is not mentally stable. She did not have a weapon, but she should not have been there. She may be a danger to herself. I also have not seen my husband who should have been the only one in my home. I know this all sounds crazy but, I left them…her there. I drove myself to the hospital. Please can you have an officer check on my home and make sure that my husband is not hurt. His name is Treyvion Stewart. Yes, I am at Mercy Medical Center. I'm ok and no I don't need to hold on to the line. Thank you."

It's been weeks since that phone call. Alexia was still trying to compartmentalize how her life had turned upside down within a few weeks. Trey was found bound in their garage with a head injury. Thankfully, he was alive. He'd been tied up in the garage for what they believe to be three days, since that is how long Tanya said she was in their home waiting for her. He suffered some short-term memory loss, but things were coming to him in pieces each day. The doctors were expecting him to make a full recovery. The baby survived as well. He was getting stronger each day and due to be released from the hospital soon.

Brenden had authorized a paternity test and he was indeed Trey's. Though Brenden was on the birth certificate, he decided that he did not want anything to do with the baby. He was driving himself crazy trying to find Tanya and getting Lex to forgive him. No one had seen Tanya since that night Lex had found them in their house. She vanished without a trace. Lex sometimes questioned had she really been there. If it wasn't for the room being changed into a makeshift nursery, she might have believed that she dreamed it all. Well, that and baby Trenton. She started to question her own sanity in the weeks that followed.

Brenden kept reaching out to her relentlessly. But she refused his calls and eventually changed her number. Lisa had come to her rescue when she called broken trying to hold on to a shred of sanity. Lisa moved in and helped her with Trey and the kids. She told Trey everything that transpired but he kept saying that it all sounded like a movie they'd seen before. It would have been nice if it were. Seeing him near death made her realize that she loved him with all her heart.

Despite everything that they had gone through, he was her best friend. She held on to that in the days when she cared for him. She had to shut out the years of pain and the chaos of the last few weeks. Her mind could not take it all in right now. Her focus was on her family. Though she hated to admit it. She had fallen in love with little Trenten. She visited him daily. How could she turn her back on a baby that didn't ask to come here? She couldn't allow him to go into the system. But that was all for another day. Trey was not able to make any legal decisions since he was considered medically incompetent for now. Though he was the biological father, she already knew that they would be raising this baby. She wondered if Tanya was alive. She had a mental breakdown that stemmed from postpartum depression and a lifelong history of bipolar disease, Lex learned from Brenden that night at the hospital. Brenden was only a distant memory. Their weekend together was a small part of heaven that she was able to enjoy. But it was both her and Trey's affairs that left them paying a lifetime debt. She was unsure if she would be able to rebound from it all anytime soon. She could only take it one day at a time. Lisa, her mother, and her children were her rock right now. She did not know how she and Trey were going to make it. But for now, she would continue to be the loving, caring, and dutiful wife that she had spent years being. She pushed her feelings aside while caring for everyone else. It was the only way that she knew how to be.

Tonight, she would be Trina. She had several personas and was able to live out her wildest fantasies here. Her hair tonight waist long and blond. She was enjoying life. She rarely thought of Brenden or Trenten these days. She was sure that Trey and Lex were taking good care of her baby. She wasn't cut out for parenthood and knew they would provide him a better life.

Brenden was another story. She did love him, but all she ever did was hurt him. She didn't deserve him. He was perfect in every sense. But that was the problem. She didn't want perfection and it would never be enough. She knew that she had hurt him beyond repair with Trenten. She wanted him to be his but always knew that he wasn't. It was a little bump in the road because she never wanted children. After Trenten she knew that her and Brenden's relation was irreparable. No one could fully love her because she could never return the feeling. It was just a word. A form of control and attachment. It wasn't something that she could help with. She never felt anything for anyone. She sought out any kind of emotion from others and craved attention, good or bad.

Sex was her outlet. She was not wife material, nor did she want to be. Now Club Creed was everything. She was introduced to it while she was street walking from city to city. It was a far cry from giving head jobs and screwing in alleys and backseats. She made good money and that provided the girls with an apartment. The tips and gifts were generous. Her regular clients took her on vacations and spoiled her. As with anything, there was a dark side. But even this she enjoyed. She had mastered being who others wanted her to be. She was also a great actress because they believed it.

From Ruby, a redheaded slut that wore plumping stained lips to Kallie, a blue-eyed want to be a country girl she could be anyone. Carla was a hit for several men. Hoodrat, ghetto, and ratchet. She wore large gold hoop earrings and popped gum. She kept a large bag full of tricks. To think Carla was called on mostly by older white gentlemen who had the perfect wife at home. One officer called on her at least once a week. He was nearing retirement and kept proposing to her. Except that he was already married to a southern bell who she was sure would drop dead if she knew the things that he did with Carla. He liked cuffing her and he was rough.

After hurting her he'd spend the rest of their time apologizing letting her dominate him. He enjoyed being spanked and whipped and would cry when she called him a bad boy. The sex was on another level. He had some serious issues mommy issues. But then again, they all had to, to keep coming back to Club Creed and enjoy it.

Stay tuned for Tanya's story in "Imperfect Fit"…

Jaded

The slam of the door echoes in Jade's ears and his voice pierces her again and again. It was as if it was on repeat in her head. She whimpers "he doesn't love me anymore." How could the man that once adored her call her fat, boring, and disgusting? Tears ran down her face. She was tired of trying. She had put so much time and effort into her makeup and hair. She was beyond hurt, frustrated, and horny as hell! He hadn't touched her in months. Every time she went out of her way for him and turn up the heat, he would shoot her down. She poured herself another glass of wine and settled down for another night alone.

Who knows what time he'd return home. She was working on her 4th or maybe 5th glass of wine when she heard a tap at the door. She opened the door and Trevor stood leaning on the frame. "Where's my boy?" She walks away leaving the door open. She grabbed the bottle of wine and decided that the bottle would be better than the glass anyway. Shrugging her shoulders, she says, "He's supposed to be with you. But obviously, he isn't since you are here." Trevor and Jordan have been boys for as long as they could remember and grew up inseparable. Trevor had been their best man, their counselor, and a best friend to her as well. She sometimes wondered if the two of them had a thing for each other. Maybe that was it. Maybe that was why Jordan wasn't attracted to her anymore. His ass was gay. That had to be it she thought, turning to Trevor.

"Am I ugly Trevor?" He looked up at her rolling his eyes. "Ok, I can see you've had enough to drink. Let me get that bottle." He reaches for the bottle and she leans forward without thinking. She ran her fingers down the center of her chest emphasizing her cleavage lifting breasts in both hands. "Are my breast too big?", turning around slowly... "what about my ass?" She jiggles it a little. "too big?" She runs her hands across her butt, trying to look back at it. "Your boy seems to think so. He says he doesn't love me anymore, that I am boring. I beg to differ. What do you think?"

She looks back at him and he is leaning on the counter staring at her ass. She walked over to the shelf and turned on her playlist. The music filled the small room. Well since her man did not want her show. Maybe Trevor would enjoy it. She danced slowly and seductively. To hell with Jordan. She knew that she still had it. Trevor was still standing in the same spot. He hadn't taken his eyes off her. She slowly began to undress, watching him watch her. She slowly undid her top, letting it fall to her waist. She knew that he wanted her. It wasn't cheating if he didn't touch her, was it?

"Tell me that you don't like what you see? She began sucking on her middle finger. One then two. She proceeds to sit down on the chaise. "Come here baby", she pats the seat next to her. He walks slowly towards her and stops in front of her. He looked afraid to come any closer.

For a minute Trevor was stuck. But, in the back of his mind, he was thinking what in the fuck is going on? Jade was gorgeous. A blind man could see that. He didn't know what the hell was going on with Jordan, but a man could only take so much. It wasn't the first time that she had hit on him, but she was getting bolder and bolder. Jordan better get his girl. Though he always knew she was too good for Jordan, but that is who she wanted.

"Tell me I'm beautiful." "You are beautiful, Jade." "Do you want me?" He had to put a stop to this. At least that's what he kept telling himself. But he hadn't moved to do so. He did want her. If the tightening in his pants wasn't a confirmation. She was watching him with her cat-like eyes. She had done something that made her golden brown and green eyes stand out. He was outside and heard their argument. He watched Jordan leave. He knew that he would be gone for hours. He took a deep breath and tried to cover her with her top.

"Come on Jade. Quit playing." She placed her fingers on his lips. Circling him she pushes him down on the chaise. The music and the wine gave her more confidence. Trevor was cute. Not as fine as Jordan but cute. He had the brains while Jordan had the brawn. She didn't understand why she overlooked him. He would have treated her like the queen that she knew she was.

Jade was the full package. She was full-figured, just the way he liked. Her light skin tone and hazel and green eyes kept heads turning. Hence the name Jade. Growing up she was quiet and shy. He always felt that she was too self-conscious. Her weight would go up and down as she tried fad diets and drinks.

She always crushed on Jordan, though she wasn't his type. It was Trevor that hooked her up with Jordan. He regretted ever doing so because he always had a thing for her. She just never showed any interest in him. Jordan was constantly dogging her from the beginning. But she seemed to like it. It was depressing. The sad thing was she was smart. She was on her game until she allowed Jordan to get into her head. Trevor constantly tried to get Jordan to see that he had a good woman and that he was dead wrong for the way that he treated her. But, with Jordan, you couldn't tell him anything.

"What the fuck" they both turned around, Jordan was standing in the opened doorway. "Aye man what the fuck is going on here?" Jordan storms up to Trevor grabbing the front of his shirt. Jade rolls her eyes and walks off leaving him to deal with Jordan. "Yo, are you for real right now? Tell me my eyes playing tricks on me." Trevor stands pushing Jordan off him. "You need to get up off me and go handle your chic. You know me better than that." "Then what the fuck are you doing up in my shit?" His voice rising with each word. "I'm not going to tell you again bro. Jade is wasted man. I don't know if she thought I was you or what, but I was trying to cover her ass up. I was not doing anything with your girl. All ya'll mother fuckers tripping. But if she keeps coming at me and your ass keeps disappearing, I may need to give both of you what the fuck ya'll asking for. Better me than some fuck nigga. Get the fuck out of here." shaking his head he walks to the door. "Didn't know you cared either way, at one time you were trying to pass her off to me."

Trevor drove mindlessly for hours. He didn't know what the fuck he was thinking. Or Jade for that matter. He had plenty of time to stop her, but damn…what man could stop that. He hardened just thinking about it. He wondered how far it would have gone if Jordan hadn't walked in. He couldn't be too sure that he would have stopped her. Hell, he didn't even realize that he hadn't shut the damn door behind him. He was sick of being in the middle of Jade and Jordan's sick love triangle. His phone kept vibrating. Between Jordan and Jade, his phone had rung every 15 minutes for the last hour. This time it was Jade. He picked up.

"This mother fucker hit me, Trevor." She was screaming in his ears. "He hit me!" He spun around without a second thought. "Where are you? Where the fuck is he? His line beeped and it was Jordan. He switched over. "Man, tell me you didn't hit her Jords?" "Man, she called you?" "I asked you a question Jordan. Man, where the hell you at?" "I left the house man. Before I killed that bitch. She runs her mother fucking mouth too much. I know that tramp tried to come on to you. I know my boy would never!" Trevor hung up on him, switching back over to Jade.

"Where are you? Jade? Hello?" He was breaking speed limits trying to get to her. He was going to fuck up Jordan. He reached their house in record time. He walked in not even knocking. "Jade?" he walked through the house. "Jade!" He called her phone again.

He heard her phone ringing following the sound. He found her in their bedroom on the floor. She had a bottle of pills in her hand popping them like candy and drinking from the same wine bottle crying.

"I can't believe he hit me. All I do for him and he treats me like trash. I gave up everything for him!" She tried to shove a handful of pills into her mouth, but Trevor grabs her hands. She yanked away from him and all the pills fall scattered on the floor. "What the hell is this Jade? He picks up the bottle, but there is no label. She was scrambling to pick them up.

"It's not worth it. I don't want to live anymore." He kicks at the pills on the floor and grabs her pulling her from the room. She goes crazy screaming and hitting him. "Let me go! It is for the best! No one wants me. No one cares!" "You're wrong. You're wrong. I care." With reluctance, he adds. "Jordan cares. He just doesn't know how to show it." He reaches for her chin and lifts it. "Where did he hit you?

Are you hurt?" He held her in his arms letting her cry it out. "Come on let's go." This wasn't the first time he had come to get her after one of their fights. He would usually drop her off at a hotel or over to one of her friends. But this time he drove home. This was the first time that Jordan had hit her, as far as he knew.

She was asleep when he got home. He wondered how many X pills she'd taken. He felt wrist. She was hot, not clammy, or sweaty and her pulse was steady. He woke her gently. "Jade" he called out to her softly. Her gorgeous eyes fluttered open. She smiled up at him, before closing her eyes again.

"Trevor, you always saving me." "It's ok. Come on. You can crash here tonight. He opens the door for her and leads her up to his driveway. His phone buzzes and he is sure it is Jordan. He opens the front door and almost carries her to the guest room. He goes into the adjoining bath of the guest and turns the shower on cold. "Come on, get in." He wasn't sure if this would be effective, but he'd seen it in movies, so it was worth a shot. Jade had already begun to undress.

"Wait...damn...wait." He notices a bruise on her upper arm. He touched her arm. "Did he do this?" The bruise erased any desire he may have had before. He felt his anger building. "Get in the shower, try not to drown yourself. I'll be back." he walked out mumbling. He closed the door to the bathroom then the bedroom. He dialed Jordan's number. "Bro…" He cut him off. "Don't bro me." His voice was cold. "You hitting on females now? Leaving bruises and shit?"

"Man, bro she's gone. I came back to check on her and she's gone. Man, I'm worried. There are pills and shit all over the floor. She left her purse, her phone. Everything man, I'm worried." Jordan was rambling. "So, you just gonna ignore me? You a woman beater now? Trevor shouted. "Man, what the fuck? My nigga what the fuck is wrong with you dog. Did you not just hear me?" "No worries, I'll be right there." Trevor hung up the phone.

He called his sister Leah. Leah was a nurse. They constantly called on her for free medical advice. She'd laugh and tell them ya'll know I'm just a nurse, right? Her passion was addiction medicine. They grew up in a home where both parents were strung out on crack and drank every and anything. They always used them as their personal punching bag. No one knew because they learned at a young age to hide the bruises. Jordan took care of her when they were kids, their roles reversing when they became older. He was rough as a teen. He stayed in the streets, gangbanging (so he thought) and he drank heavily. He never touched any drugs though. He and Jordan would stay out all night. They frequently got into fights. Leah would always be the one to patch the two of them up after one of their brawls. He'd stopped abruptly one night when she confided in him that she was scared. His father was locked up and their mother had died of an overdose. She didn't want to end up in foster care. Trevor was 18 and responsible for her. If something happened to him, she would be left alone. He couldn't do that to her. Who would take care of her if he followed in their footsteps? He never took another drink after that night. He got a real job started taking night classes. He promised her that they would be better than their parents. She was 16 years old. He made sure that she finished school at the top of her class.

　　"Hello?" Leah answered after a few rings. "Lea I need you to go to the house. I need you to check on Jade." "What's Jade doing at your place?" "Her and Jordan got into. He banged her up a little." "He did what?!" "You heard me, but that's not it. I found her with a bottle of X. She was popping them joints like candy. I don't know how many she took."

"And you left her?!" "Lea just, listen ok. I took her back to my place. She was awake, coherent. I told her to jump in the shower. It was cold. She was maybe a little loopy, but she wasn't half dead. Can you please just go by and check on her?" "I'm already on my way. I'll be there in a few and I'll call you when I get there." They hung up as he turned the corner.

Trevor pulled into Jordan's driveway. He made his way up the pavement quickly. When he reached the door, Jordan was peeking out of the window. He opened the door. "Man, I'm glad to see- "Trevor didn't let him finish his sentence hitting him in the mouth drawing blood. "What the fuck!" Jordan swung back but his swing was off. He smelled of liquor and swayed off-balanced. He tried to swing again, but Trevor avoided his fist and punched him in the gut. It wasn't the first time he and Jordan fought. Jordan usually could hold his own, and he felt a little bad because he knew he was lit. But he couldn't stop. "I'm going to fuck your bitch as up." His mind flashing back to the many nights he and Leah hid under the bed or in the closet trying to escape their parents fighting. He kicked Jordan and he grunted. "I ought to kill you, but you aren't even worth it. She's at my place and if you think of coming near her I just might." With that, he walked off. This was not how he expected his night to turn out. This night started off bad from the moment Jade came on to him. The fact that for a second, he enjoyed it, made him angrier. He was now kicking himself for it. How many pills had she taken before he got there?

That would explain why she was behaving the way she did. His phone buzzed and he picked up mid-ring. "Lea, is she ok?" "Yea I'm here. She's ok. Her blood pressure and pulse are a little high but normal and her oxygen is 100%. Which is good. She vomited a few times before I got here, and it had some undigested pills in it." His stomach turned a little. Lea was the one good with cleaning up puke and stuff. She usually took care of their parents when they had had too much. She would nurse them through the cycles of binging and withdrawals. He never had the stomach for that stuff. "Ok good so that means she's good?" "I believe so, I'll stay the night to keep an eye on her."

"I have to be to work at 7 so your gonna have to take off and stay with her tomorrow." "Ok cool". It was just as it was growing up. They took turns missing school to "watch" their parents when things got really bad. "Thanks sis. I'm almost to the house. I had to have some words with Jordan. Man, I couldn't let that shit go. This has been a crazy night. Jade doesn't deserve any of this shit man. She's a good girl. I should have intervened a long time ago."

"It's not your fault Trevor and I doubt you could convince her or Jordan to do anything. You know how this goes. It's just another form of addiction. She's addicted to him and he to her. One of them must get enough to make a change. There's nothing that you or anyone else can do about it. The more you push the more you'll push her away. All you can do is be there for her and him." "Man fuck him".

"Yea you say that now...Is that you to the door?" "Yea it's me." He hangs up and meets Lea in the hall. "She's asleep." Leah waves him towards the living room. "Ok fill me in on everything." "Lea shit was crazy. Jordan hit me up earlier tonight on some fuck shit. He was talking crazy. He must have been on some shit. He called saying how he was sick of Jade and shit. Calling her out of her name and saying how she was fat and ugly."

"All the while she was there because I could hear her in the background." Leah's jaw drops. "I'm telling you. Then he starts talking about some chick he's been fucking with and said he was going over there for the night. He told Jade he was going to crash at my place. He was really on another level. So, I ran by there to check on her. I was outside and could hear them arguing upstairs." He settles on the couch and Lea's hanging on to every word.

"So, when he pulled out, I went upstairs to check on her right." Leah shakes her head up and down. "Well, when I walk in, she's on some shit too. Asking me if she's cute and shit. If I found her attractive." Leah's eyes widen. "She was going hard at me and for a second I lost it. I mean she was half-naked and," he shook his head. "I got caught up for a second, but then I tried stopping her. I was trying to cover her up and take the wine bottle away from her when Jordan walked in."

"WTF," Leah shakes her head "You are lying bro." "Naw I'm telling you. Both of them been tripping hard tonight. Jordan came at me accusing me of messing with Jade. I was like both of ya'll got problems and need to chill the fuck out. I just got up and left. They keep me in the middle of some mess." "Ok, so how did Jade get with you then?" "Oh, there's more" he finishes telling her the details of the night right up until he called her. "Ok, so what happened when you went to Jordan? Didn't you say that you went to see him?"

"Man, Lea I fucked his ass up. You know how I feel about a man putting his hands on a female. That shit ain't cool and he knows it. I don't even know why he called me on that fuck shit. Besides, I've been knowing Jade, longer than him. She ain't no trick he just met, she's family. We have all been running together since we were in school. She like my sis. I'm gonna be on that shit just as if a man put his hands on you. Except I really would be in jail tonight."

"But Trev that's your boy. Yall like best friends." "And? That's more of a reason to get his ass kicked. He of all people should know better. Anyways let me go check on her." "Naw I got it. You already said she was on them X. Them, joints have you thinking you a damn stripper on the pole or porn star. You already said she came on to you tonight. Let's keep you out of a situation until this shit is out of her system."

"Yea, you right. Dang Lea, do you think she might need to go to the hospital?" "No, I think she's good but I 'll keep a close eye on her tonight." He followed her to the door of the bedroom. She opened the door and Jade was naked sprawled across the bed. He turned away but had already caught an eye full.

"See what I was talking about." She quickly shut the door behind her. He could hear her through the door. "I'll just check her vitals again." He walked down the hall and waited. Leah returned a few minutes later. "I'll set my clock to check over the next few hours. But she's been steady for the last hour, so I think she'll be fine. I'll sleep in here tonight too." He handed her an extra blanket and pillow and she said she'd be fine on the futon. He went upstairs and took a shower. He tiptoed back downstairs and peaked in on them, they were both snoring lightly. Leah woke him the next morning lightly tapping on his shoulder. "Hey bro. I gotta go. I have to run by the house and change. She's good. She woke up upset a few hours ago and we talked for a while. I updated her a little, she didn't remember much. She's still sleeping now."

"Ok, thanks sis. I love you." "I love you too." Trevor got up and padded quietly downstairs. The door to the guest room was open. He paused before peeking into the doorway. Jade was fully dressed, thankfully, and still asleep. He'd catch up on some more sleep and hopefully, she would too. He headed back upstairs, then changed his mind and headed back down. He grabbed the neatly folded blanket and pillow that Leah left and quietly made a pad on the floor beside Jade.

Jade woke moaning. Her head pounded and her left shoulder ached when she turned. The sun was peeking between the blinds. Blinds that weren't hers. She sat up looking around the room. Beautiful bold African artwork hung all the walls. She stifled a yawn as the last few hours played in her mind. She was at Trevor's. She woke this morning a little disoriented and Leah had filled her. There was a glass of water and a bottle of Motrin on the bedside table. She hung her feet over the side of the bed and met a warm heap. She peered over the side of the bed and Trevor met eyes with Trevor.

"Good morning," he leaned on one arm staring at her. "How are you feeling." She shrugged, "I'm ok" before looking away. "Are you sure? No judgment here. I need to know something. Is this the first time that he's hit you?" She answered quickly, a little too quickly. "Yes…" she paused, "Well, we've got into fights before. He may have put his fingers in my face, tapped my forehead, or shoved me. But" she swallowed; her eyes filled with tears "this is the first time that he's hit me." She shook her head and rested her head in her hands. "I cannot believe this is happening. He stood on his knees placing his hand on her knee.

"I'm sorry Jade. There's no excuse for his behavior. And you should have told me the first time it happened. You do know that this is not your fault right and you do not have to put up with this." "I know, it's just." He became angry. "No just", he said maybe too harshly because she grimaced.

"Look I'm sorry. I'm probably not the best person to talk to about this. Just know that I am here for you. You can stay as long as you want or I'm sure Lea won't mind you crashing at her place for a while." "I'm really fine. He doesn't get like this often. I'll be fine. I'm going back home." "No, you're not." She looked up her eyes changing with her mood. Whenever she was angry her eyes took a darker cherry wood tone. "Excuse me?" He sighed "I'm making matters worse."

"Jade, I'm just worried about you. Could you please stay here or with Lea for a few days at least until this goes over? I'm worried about you...and Jordan. Besides, I may have made things worse." Her eyes narrowed, "what do you mean worse." He looked down this time. "Well, you kind of came on to me last night." She groaned covering her face with her hands. "Tell me I did not." "You did," he said. "What exactly did I do?"

"You don't want to know. Let's just say you had a few too many drinks, you danced a little, nothing else happened. I left but not before Jordan came home and you know the rest of the story. I went back and put my foot up his ass after I saw your arm." He stood then. Speaking of your arm, let me see it. She looked at her arm lifting the sleeve. She had a large bruise, and it was already darker than the night before.

He stood angrily. "It's really ok. It doesn't hurt that much. Plus, you know my skin is light, so it doesn't take much to leave a mark." She shrugged. "Bull shit," he reached out tracing it. "I'm sorry. You really don't deserve any of this." "Quit apologizing. You act as if you did this to me. When are you going to stop apologizing for Jordan? When are you going to stop trying to save him?" She paused staring into his eyes. "When you do." They both look away.

"Anyways, you want some breakfast?" he asked. "Sure, she replied. Lea left some clothes in the closet. I'm sure there's something that you can wear." He stood and walked out of the room. A few minutes later she could hear cabinets opening and closing. She shed a few more tears, before getting up. She walked into the bathroom.

He had a new pack of toothbrushes and toothpaste on the sink. One of the perforated ends was torn off. She wondered who else had been here using one.

Shrugging because it wasn't any of her business, she quickly brushed her teeth and washed her face. She rummaged around in the closet and found a t-shirt and shorts set. She had to settle for no underwear and the same bra for now. The clothes fit a little snug but fit, nonetheless. The smell of fried bacon reached her, and her stomach growled. She found him in the kitchen. His unkept hair was messy. Which was out of place for him because he always kept his short locs neat. Matter of fact he was always very well kept. Nothing out of order. She noticed as well that he kept his house that way as well. It was clean, a little too clean with no woman in the house. His open floor plan sported a beautiful kitchen with white cabinets and caramel-colored walls. His living room and dining walls were different shades of grey and his furniture was all dark with bold pillows that matched the artwork that hung on the walls.

It reminded her of a mini-museum. It fit him. He always had that power to the people vibe. She hadn't seen the inside of his home since he and Jordan lived together. That was several years ago before they got a place of their own. Trevor watched her as she took in his place.

She walked around for a while without saying anything. Lea's clothes hugged her curves and she had curves for days. She was a pretty girl. Even with no makeup, she was beautiful. She wore her hair short. At least he thinks it was her hair. You never could tell these days because the wigs and weaves looked so natural. She looked up and caught him watching her. She cleared her throat. "You got it smelling good up in here. I didn't know you could cook. Oh, and your house is nice."

"Yea, who you think kept Jordan fed in our college days?" When he mentioned Jordan's name her eyes saddened, and her shoulders sunk slightly. It was as if hearing his name deflated her. "You hungry?" "Yea starving." "Good, you mind setting the table. Everything is on there already." Figuring that doing something with her hands may help her to get her mind off things. He hated the defeated look in her. She was voted most likely to succeed in school. She was excited about life. It hurt to think that she may have lost that lust for life because of Jordan. Most women did not know just how much power they gave to men. If only women knew just how much power they truly held. That they could have everything in a man that they wanted because he would step up and be that if he wanted her. All she had to do was demand that upfront and not let him slide. Most men would take all she had to give up and more if she allowed him to. He schooled Lea early on. Telling her not to ever get into the habit of settling, trying to change a man, or waiting for a man to change. If he didn't have it when he came to the table, then he didn't eat.

They ate quietly. The sound of their forks ringing out against their plates. He'd made pancakes, bacon, and eggs. He had given her a heaping serving and she ate it all. She believed Jordan would be at work by now glancing at the clock above him. No matter how torn up he was the night before he'd wake up and go to work. He rarely had a hangover. He was what they called a "functioning addict." He was a heavy drinker and recently starting using pills and coke. She knew because she had found his stash. It explained his erratic behavior lately. He kept telling her that he had it under control. He claimed that he didn't need it. But things only got worse. Sometimes he would go weeks without using and those weeks they would get along great.

But when he did his mood swings were worse. His eyes changed. He'd binge for days at a time and his words and actions were becoming harsher. He was always paranoid and accusing her of sleeping around, stealing his money, or playing him as he would put it. The next morning it would be like she dreamed it all. The real Jordan would be back. He never wanted to hear about how he behaved the night before. He'd act like nothing ever happened and expected her to act the same. Always saying you can't blame a sober man for a drunk man's action.

Her thoughts made her agree, saying "I'll stay for a few days, but I need to go get my things. My phone, laptop, and some clothes." She worked from home now. It was easier and that way Jordan didn't have anyone to accuse her of messing around. Also, he couldn't come up to her Job and embarrass her. She made her schedule so she could work every day if she wanted or only a few days a week. Jordan didn't want her working but she had to have her own money. Sometimes he'd act funny with his money and she didn't have time for that shit. Besides her daddy taught her to never depend on a man or anyone to take care of her.

She didn't know when it had gotten this bad. It was as if one day she woke up in this nightmare. "I can take you to get your things and grab your car too." "I don't think that is a good idea, Trevor." "Well, then Lea can take you when she gets off. You are not going by yourself." She shrugged, he noticed that she did that a lot. "I just don't want to be a bother and if Jordan is there, I don't want you guys fighting." "Don't worry about that. Jordan is a big boy and so am I." She decided to stay after finding out that he and Jordan had fought. Though nothing has ever been between her and Trevor, Jordan would think there was now.

She needed to feel him out before going back. But she couldn't let him know that she was staying with Trevor. She wrestled with her thoughts during the ride. Jordan's car wasn't home; she sighed in relief. She didn't realize that she was holding her breath until they pulled up to their unit. "I'll be right back," she told Trevor. "I'll come up with you."

"No, Jordan's not here so I'll be ok." She jogged up the stairs to their top unit unlocking the door. She stopped at the doorway. She did not remember leaving the house this way. There was broken glass everywhere. She carefully made her way around the mess and went to the bedroom. Her phone was on the floor shattered. She ran to the closet and breathed a sigh of relief. Her laptop was untouched on the top shelf. But her makeup vanity was turned upside down, her small bottles and tubes scattered across the room. Some were broken. One wall was dusted with a variety of colors with her shadows and powders.

She fought back tears as she made her way through it all. Trevor had a habit of destroying her things, then replacing them when he was sober. She quickly packed a bag and picked up what makeup she could salvage. She walked out the front door and locked it brushing away tears. She waved at Trevor he followed behind her.

Jordan sat at his desk. He hadn't gotten any work done. He wore sunglasses to conceal his wounds. But it didn't do much, he still received numerous whistles and questions. When asked whose ass needed to be kicked, he muttered to himself "mines." He gave them a story involving him and a bar fight over the weekend. He picked up his phone for the 50th time, hoping that Jade had called. When his phone finally rang, he answered "Jade?" "Hey hun. No, it's mom. How are you doing?" "I'm fine mom," he answered. "Everything ok?" "Yea, everything is ok. I'm just running low on cash is all." "Ok, I'll put something in your account today." "Thanks son. I love you."

He nodded as if she could see him as he hung up. He'd have to stop at the apple store and get Jade a new phone. Maybe he'd get her the new 11. She'd mentioned upgrading soon. He kept her phones replaced. Little did she know he had a tracker on her phone. He had no answer to when or why he started that. But he found himself checking her whereabouts often. He needed to doing better. He didn't mean to hit her last night. He doesn't know what came over him. It was something about seeing her with Trevor. It did something to him. He knew that Trevor would never, but nothing surprised him anymore and Jade was begging for attention. He gave up on getting any work done today and decided to call it a day. It was after 3 anyway.

He stopped by the apple store and picked out a rose-colored iPhone 11 and a nice case. His second stop was to the store to pick up some roses and a card. He was going to have to work hard for her to forgive him for this one. He was surprised when he pulled in and her car wasn't in its usual spot. He went upstairs, the house was still in disarray. She couldn't have been home because she would have cleaned up the place. He walked through the house, broken glass crunching with each step. When he reached the bedroom, he realized that she had been there. Her cell phone was on the dresser, and her drawers were left open.

She had a thing about leaving things out of order. She always made the bed and the drawers had to be tightly shut.

Her computer bag was gone out of the closet as well. Maybe she went up the street to the café to get some work done. He drove by there, but her car wasn't there so headed back home and decided he'd surprise her by cleaning up the place himself.

Jade closed the laptop. She managed to get some work done today. She yawned and headed down the hall. Trevor had left earlier saying he had some things to take care of. He was good at taking care of everyone. She walked around his home exploring each room. Everything was neat and in order upstairs as well. There were 5 bedrooms total. One had been converted into an office. There were also 3 baths. Each room was vastly different but holding a common theme. His bedroom door was closed. It was the last room that she entered. She thought it may be locked, but it opened when she turned the knob. It screamed bachelor. The room alone would have a girl dropping her panties. It held a king-size bed with large posts on all 4 corners.

A provocative African American tapestry hung above the head of the bed. It was a black and white portrait of a naked couple. Her breast was covered by her hands, their bodies intricately entwined. The picture said a lot. A large picture hung on another wall. The words *fuck it just get naked* stood out against the deep wood grain. Trevor obviously had a side to him she'd never seen. She touched his sheets, they were silk. Black silk. Covered with a black and gold oversized comforter. She imagined how it would feel to lay in his bed. He had an array of colognes and body sprays on his dresser. A picture of him and Leah and one of their parents were the only family photos she had seen in the whole house. She opened a few drawers. Everything was folded neatly, and each drawer was categorized. She decided that she had seen enough and felt she was borderline snooping. She closed the door behind her and headed back downstairs.

Trevor watched her on his camera. He didn't mean to, but her movement turned on the camera and alerted his phone. There was one at every entrance and in his bedroom. He would disable them while she was there. He envisioned her sprawled across his bed as she was last night. Naked and beneath him but stopped that train of thought abruptly getting out of his car. He walked into the house calling her name. She looked like she was caught with her hand in the cookie jar. "Hey, I was just exploring your home. I hope you don't mind," she said quickly looking away.

"You're fine," he said waving his hand. "Have you eaten since this morning?" It was the first time that she had thought about food. She frowned, "no, I haven't. He frowned as well "And why not?" "I guess I hadn't thought about it. I was working most of the day. Then I ran out to get another phone since mines were broken." "I thought you said you left it home. You didn't say it was left home broken."

"Well, it wasn't broken when I left it, as far as I know. But it sure was when I went by there this morning." "You should have told me. I would have gotten you another one." This time she waved her hand. "You didn't break it, besides it's not your responsibility."

He decided to let it go. "Ok. Well, I have some Chinese food that I picked up. It's enough for two," holding up bags. He headed towards the kitchen and she followed. He set the Styrofoam containers out across his kitchen island and allowed her to fix her food first.

"Do you mind if I take it to my-, I mean the guest room?" "No, you're fine." She headed to the room and closed the door, trying to put some distance between them. She still did not think it was a good idea to be there and if Jordan found out there would be hell to pay. But it was better to pay it here, than back at their place alone. She rubbed and her neck, thinking of how he choked her almost to the point of passing out. She knew that Trevor wouldn't let anything happen to her. She was grateful for him and Leah over the years. Besides Jordan, they were the only family she had here. She'd have to stop in and thank Leah for taking care of her the other night. She didn't drink often, for obvious reasons, and didn't know why she took Jordan's pills. She didn't intend on taking any. She began tossing them out around the room so that he would find them.

She ended up pouring wine on them so that he wouldn't be able to pick them up and use them. Curiosity got the best of her and she took one, then another. Once she had a nice buzz going, she stopped. She wasn't sure when that lead to her thinking about taking the whole bottle, a good thing Trevor walked in then. She initially wanted to see all the hype was about, but never again.

Her voicemail was full, and she had multiple text messages from Jordan. She did read the first few which consisted mostly of *where are you? When are you coming home? I'm sorry. I love you.* Further down his tone had changed. One message starting out *Bitch*! She dropped her phone on the bed deciding to not read the rest.

She was sick of the roller coaster of emotions he kept her on. She decided to turn off her phone and watch TV. A reality show on strippers was on. She watched it, but her mind was elsewhere. She got up to put away her dishes. What Trevor called enough for two was enough for 4. She was stuffed. He'd already cleaned up the kitchen and headed upstairs to his room. She washed the dishes she used and went back to the guest room. She could hear the faint sounds of whistles coming from his room. He must be watching a game. She went back to her room closing the door.

Jordan was really pissed now. He sat in their dark home downing one beer after another. When he had enough, he switched to the bottle of liquor. Where the fuck was Jade? This was the first time she ever stayed from home this long. Her phone was going straight to voicemail.

He thought she may have gone to Leah's place but couldn't bring himself to call her. He knew by now that Trevor had told her everything. He was too ashamed to call, and Leah would surely get on him more than Trevor had. He knew eventually he would have to hear it, but he wasn't feeling like it tonight. He smoked on a joint. He thought about riding by Leah's place, but he was already on Trevor's shit list. If he found out he was stalking Leah's place it would only make things worse. He'd give her until tomorrow. But she better be walking her ass up in here tomorrow. He didn't play that sleeping out shit.

A week had passed, and Jade was beginning to miss her own space. Trevor was very accommodating, and Leah stopped by every evening and hung out with her.

They would talk for hours. Trevor was avoiding her. She would only see him in passing and she felt he was spending more time away because she was there. She didn't want him feeling put out of his own place. It was past time for her to go home. She'd finally responded to Jordan when his texts started showing that he was really worried about her. She only meant to let him know that she was ok. But that only added another crack in her shield. She eventually read every text and had listened to every voicemail. All of which were from Jordan. He begged her to pick up and she reluctantly did. They talked for a while.

He kept apologizing and promising that it wouldn't happen again. He even agreed to counseling. She wouldn't tell him where she was staying. Only that she was with a friend and safe. Later that day she handed Trevor his spare key thanking him, but she was ready to go home. He only asked her once to stay, but she had made up her mind. She felt that she had worn out her welcome and she was missing Jordan. She hugged Trevor, kissed him on the cheek, and left.

Jordan watched Jade come up the driveway. She was cute in her green romper and sandals. She wore her hair curly and short today. He used to love the versatility of her hairstyles and makeup. Come to think of it, he hadn't complimented her in a long time. He did so when she reached the door. "I like what you have on. It looks good on you. You look good." She looked up surprised and smiled at him. He reached for her bag and waited for her to come in. He hoped she liked the new furniture he'd gotten and her new vanity table.

A new designer bag and matching shoes were on her chair waiting for her as well. He waited for her usual squeal of laughter when he bought her new things, but she barely looked at any of them. He frowned. "What's wrong baby? You don't like it?" She turned reassuring him. "No, I love it. But look Jordan we need to talk." "I know, I know baby. I fucked up. I don't know how many ways I can say I'm sorry." "Yeah sure, I hear you. But the thing is you can say it a million times, but it means nothing if you don't show me."

He walked up to her gathering her in his arms. "I am showing you, well I'm trying to show you. Just wait and see." He kissed her but she pulled back, throwing him off. She never rejected him, most of the time she was begging him to touch her. "What? So now I can't kiss you?" She put some distance between them. At least that was the way it felt. "So, who's house you said you stayed at again?"

"I never said." "My point. The way your acting got me questioning who you've been with." "Look Jordan, maybe this wasn't a good idea. I think we need a break. I can't keep doing this" she threw up her hands heading towards the door. She barely heard him mutter, "so you just gonna leave me like everybody else. I thought you said you would never leave me?"

She stopped looking back at him. He genuinely appeared hurt and lost. "Damn, baby how many times do I have to say I'm sorry? He pleaded. "Just give me one more chance to show you. I do love you and I never meant to hurt you. You know I'd never put my hands on you. It was the pills. I'm done with them. I'm done smoking. I'll stop it all for you. Just give me another chance." He whispered, "baby please."

He held out his hand and she dropped her bags and went to him. She went into his arms hugging him. He held her tightly nuzzling her neck. "I swear I'd never hurt you baby." She felt the moisture of tears before sniffling, pulling at

her heartstrings. He rarely cried. He rarely showed any emotion other than anger lately. "Baby you have to open up and talk to me. I don't know what is happening to us, to you." He gripped her tighter. "I know, I know." They stood that way rocking back and forth. Eventually, he moved away from her, dashing his tears away. "You hungry? We can go out if you want."

"Naw, I'm good." She was tired of him calling her fat. She had decided that maybe it wasn't such a bad idea to try losing some weight. "Well, we can order in. Watch some movies if you'd like." "Sure, that sounds good." Jordon called one of her favorite restaurants and ordered. She turned on the television, flipping through Netflix's new releases. They settled on a movie that she had begged him to take her to the theater to see. But as usual, he was too busy. He set them up on the floor picnic-style and they got comfortable. They were midway through the movie when their food arrived. Jordan jumped up to answer the door. While he was up she paused their show as her phone vibrated. It was Leah checking up on her. She quickly let her know that she was good and set the phone down. Jordan grabbed some candles out of the cabinet and a tray setting them up. Once done he dimmed the lights and settled next to her. They ate silently, watching the television. She only picked at her food before pushing it away. Jordan noticed and asked, "that's all your eating" You love Sista Soulja's." "I do" she replied, "but I'm not hungry." "So, who were you texting a few minutes ago?" he asked, sliding her phone over. "It was just Leah checking in on me."

"Oh, so ya'll cool like that now?" he asked. She shrugged her shoulder. "I've missed hanging out with Leah and my friends. She was checking up on me." "Oh, so you were over to her place?" "Look Jordan" her mood changing. "I wasn't to anyone's house ok. I rented a place and took some time to myself."

He didn't want to piss her off, so he let it go for now. He got up and went to the room and grabbed a gift bag. "Hey, I'm sorry about your phone. I swear I must have blacked out the other night. You know that isn't me. I see you got yourself another phone. I guess you would have had to for work. Anyways. I had already picked up another one, but you never came home." She opened it and smiled. "I knew you wanted one babe." Smiling in relief. "You see I do be listening to you." "Thanks, but." "No buts, you can keep yours as a standby." "We don't need to the extra expense. I'm cool with this prepaid phone. You really should take it back." "Nonsense, I got you babe. I planned on getting you one for your birthday anyways."

She tucked it all back in the bag neatly and set it aside. "Let's just finish the movie." Jordan wasn't interested in the movie she picked out. She loved watching those fake love stories. He had tuned out long ago and decided to watch her instead. She was trying to play hard, but he knew better. He liked how she wore her hair. The short styles were cute on her. Not those long curly wigs and weaves she liked wearing. She was a beautiful girl, she just needed to shed a few pounds. Her ass drew too much attention. He crawled closer to her. Fuck this standoff attitude she had. He knew exactly how to have her eating out of his hand. He pictured those thick legs up on his shoulders. She was flexible despite her size. He was thinking of just how flexible when she turned to look at him.

"What?" she asked smiling at him. She knew exactly what he wanted. "You know good and damn well you ain't watching that shit. Get on over here. I missed you baby. You know you can't be up and leaving me for as long as you did." He crawled over here. "I got something else better for you to see." "Oh, yea?" She laughed kissing him back. "Thank you for my gifts daddy," she said seductively.

"You're welcome. I know the perfect way you can show your appreciation." The movie has long forgotten he showed her just who belonged to. The next few weeks were great. Jordan never left her side other than to go to work. He had even taken off a few days to "work on them". He brought her gifts every day. Stuffed animals, clothing, and lots of lingerie. They had more sex in those few days than they had in the last year. She wasn't sure what he was trying to prove but, but she was enjoying every minute of it. Her body on the other hand was telling her to slow it down. Her body ached inside and out. She didn't know how much more her girl could take. She hadn't heard from Trevor since going back home. She wondered if he was upset with her. She knew she shouldn't have taken Jordan back after he'd hit her. But he'd never done it before, and he promised that he wouldn't again. It was that stuff he was on that had him acting out. He had been clean for weeks now. No drugs or alcohol. He was working hard on turning over a new leaf. But deep down she wondered how long it would last.

It wasn't long before she noticed him coming home later and later. He told her that he was hanging out with his boys after work, that was all. One night he stumbled through the front door. He was upset, arguing with himself for having too much to drink. "I swear I didn't mean to get fucked up Jade. I just need to sleep it off" he mumbled. She helped him to bed. He kept talking about how he was going to put it on her, pulling at her clothes. He stunk of cigarettes and alcohol. She told him he needed a shower and ran the water for him. But he never made it out of the bed. She lingered in the shower as he shouted, "Baby hurry big daddy's waiting on you!" She stayed in the shower until the water ran cold. Having sex with him drunk was not a fun experience. She spent most of the time trying to get him up.

Thankfully, he was fast asleep when she came back into the room. She crawled in next to him and he pulled her to him. She lay still until his grip loosened and she heard him snoring again. He was gone when she woke. He called later that morning apologizing about last night. "You see I didn't come in bothering you last night, did I? I told you I was good. I had a few drinks, but I swear that was all." They chatted for a few minutes and hung up.

She decided to spend the day at the spa. She splurged a little and pampered herself. She was going out with Leah and some friends that evening. They had to beg her to join them for drinks.

Jade was working hard at losing weight. She was walking for an hour every day and wanted to get a gym membership. She glanced at herself in the mirror. She hadn't lost any pounds, but she was sure she was a little slimmer in the waist. She turned in the mirror admiring her outfit. She sported a black keyhole top with the slit sleeves and fitted, ripped denim. It was warming up, so she didn't wear much makeup and wore her hair tapered with curls on the top. She was slipping on her sandals when Jordan walked in.
He whistled when he saw her. "Where do you think you're going?"

"I don't think I'm going anywhere. I'm going," she said with emphasis, "out with Leah and friends." "Well, you didn't tell me you were going anywhere." "Because I wasn't planning on going. But since you're going out again tonight, I decided to take them up on the offer." "We were just gonna watch the game, you could come with me. You had to get all dressed up to go with Leah? Where are ya'll going?" He wasn't sure why he was irritated. "What time do you think you'll be back? I'm not going to be out that late. I had planned on spending this evening with you. He reached for her hand pulling her up against him. He nudged her ear. "I bought this thing I saw online. It's these straps that you get into and it hangs from the door. So, I can…" he demonstrated humping her leg. "Me? Hanging off one of these doors? She raised an eyebrow. Hell naw, you'll be picking up the door and me off the floor!" "Don't worry, I got you. I can hold you up baby." He tried undoing her zipper. "Matter of fact we can skip all that bullshit and get it out of the clothes right now."

She laughed wiggling out of his grip. "No, you don't! I'll see you later. I hope these straps thick. It's going to need to be to hold up all of this" slapping her thighs! "Cause you see I don't need none of those play shits made for them skinny ass girls. I'm all woman here," she said moving her hips in sync with her words.

He was already unbuttoning his shirt. But she grabbed her keys and headed towards the door. "Damn baby, you gonna leave a nigga here begging?" "Never that. You don't even have to beg for what is already all yours." With that, she blew him a kiss and opened the door closing it softly behind her. He stood watching her walk down the stairs. Shit, she did just leave him. That was a first. Oh well, she'd pay for it tonight when he had her up in the straps. Fuck it and went to take a shower. He dressed thinking I can get down just as well as she could. He took his time finding the right outfit. He decided on a dark grey fitted shirt that hugged his biceps and dark gray jeans that fit him just right. He decided to stop by the barbershop to get a trim line and his face cleaned up. He shot Jade a picture and sent a text. *You sure you want to be leaving all this tonight to go out with yo girls?* He waited for her response. She didn't reply immediately as she always did. As he pulled up to his favorite spot his phone chimed. He opened the text, but she only replied *mmmmhhh.*

He smiled before jumping out. He had to make sure she knew what she had at home. He sent her another quick text with him licking his lips. *See I could be licking something else, but you go ahead with your girls. Make sure you bring it back for me tonight.* With that, he turned off his phone and decided to go have himself a good time. He didn't have anything to worry about. She needed to get out from time to time. Maybe she would nag him less if she found something to do. The bar was crowded. Several shouted at him when he walked in. "Jordan what's up man!" "Jordan"

He was smiling until he met eyes with Trevor. He knew eventually he was going to run into him. He nodded his head in his direction. "Trev", "Jordan." The tension was thick enough to cut between them. The fellas looked back and forth. "How have you been man?" He treaded lightly not sure where they stood. They'd gotten into many times over the years, but never over a female. Hell, they'd share them or enjoy a good competition, but at the end of the day, they were boys. Trevor raised his eyebrow before shrugging him off. He turned to grab the small cube chalking his stick. to He leaned on the table looking back at Jordan after an uncomfortable pause.

"I'm good. Yo who's up man?" No one answered him as the tension in the air increased a notch. "What's good, ya'll two alright?" one of the guys asked. "I don't know, are we?" Trevor shot at Jordan. "Just as long as we have an understanding, I'm good here." Jordan shook it off. Man, Trevor was his boy, and he was the one that fucked up.

"Man, we good" he lifted his fist and Trevor bumped fists with him. 'Aye let me get a drink for my boy," Trevor raised his hand towards the bar. "Now let's shoot some pool." After several rounds of drinks and games, everyone was mellowed. Jordan ordered some wings, and they were all focused on the game. Several were shouting out others quietly watching.

Jordan headed outside to the smoking area. After a few minutes, Trevor followed him. There was a nice breeze outside. Trevor cleared his throat. "So, how's Jade." "She's good. We're good Trev. I know I crossed the line man. I don't know what the hell came over me. You know I'd never hurt her. I know how you feel about all that shit man. Hell, how many niggas we've roughed up over the years if we even thought one of them had pushed around Leah or any other girls. I'm no woman beater man."

"Then tell me what exactly is going on with you? Leah said Jade had told her you fucking with powder now. Jordan, you know that shit ain't nothing but the devil." "Naw man. I ain't fucking with that shit. I may pop a couple of pills now and then just to take the edge off but that's it man I swear. I left that shit alone too. I'm about to leave it all alone. These cigs" as he smashed the butt into the small collection of gravel tossing it into the small opening. "I gotta get my head right man. The drinking, smoking, pills all man." "Word man."

"I don't like what's it's doing to you man. I've been hearing some shit for a while, but I tried to step back and let you handle your shit." "I'm a good man. Are we good?" he asked Trevor. "Yeah man, like I said we good. Man take care of yourself and Jade. She loves the hell out of you and brings the best out in you man."

"Stop all this bullshit! Yall should have been married already working on some little brats." "Oh yeah, and what about you man? Where your damn rug rats at?" "Shit, I ain't found anyone worthy of my seeds. All in time. But you and Jade, ya'll made for each other man. Yall been at this for a long time. These females out here man. Ain't worth shit. I mean don't get me wrong, I enjoy them." He smiled, a faraway look in his eyes.

"Hell yeah, but ain't none of them wife material. I ain't got anyone waiting for me to come home. Have a meal cooked for me. Shit. You got it, man." Their conversation was still on his mind as Trevor drove home. Shit, he was tired of going home to an empty house. He was ready to settle down. He just hadn't met anyone that was on his level. A big old empty ass house wasn't all it was caked up to be. His thoughts taking him back to the small filthy apartment they grew up in. He and Leah tried to keep the place clean, but it was a shit hole. His folks stayed breaking things. The carpets and walls were dingy. He learned to appreciate things over the years. Especially things that were his. That's why he took such extra care of his things. When you never had shit. You learned to appreciate it.

Jordan made it home before Jade. He was feeling good but wasn't drunk. He'd sent her a message asking where she was, but she hadn't responded. He didn't like this shit. He knew she was still upset but, damn. His phone chimed and he picked it up thinking that it was Jade. Instead, it was Courtney. Courtney was a pretty little thing he saw from time to time. He'd met while traveling for work. She'd stop through whenever she was in town. It had been a minute since they hooked up. He hesitated before opening the text. Damn. She'd sent a pic of her bent over across the bed. Her ass was the first he saw, she was looking back at the camera with this sexy ass smile on her face. Another text followed with a local address. These girls knew how to put a nigga in a situation. He looked at the time. It was 2 am.

His boy downstairs was already waking up after seeing Courtney's ass sprawled out across his screen. Shit not only was Courtney a freak she was fine as hell. He sat rubbing himself. Thinking he'd just relieve himself until Jade got home. But, by 230 he'd long since stopped and had taken a cold shower.

Jade knew that Jordan would be pissed. He always started an argument whenever she went out. He didn't as much today. She intentionally stayed out late. Let him see how it felt to be at home waiting on her for a change. She had to force herself to not keep checking her phone for the onslaught of messages that was sure to come from Jordan. He had texted a few times but so far, no voicemails. That was much better than the 20 or so she was used to. At the end of the night, they all decided to go back to Leah's place. Jade had maybe one too many drinks and sat back watching Leah and her friends continue their party. She was bored hours ago but tried to entertain them by hanging. She was tired and was thinking about how good her bed would feel right about now. But no one was in the condition to drive her home. She thought about calling Jordan, but she wanted him to think that she was having the time of her life.

The girls were pouring another round of shots and hollering "shots, shots, shots."

"Come on Jade. Put that damn phone down and come get one of these," Tiff yelled. Tiff was already swaying as Jade thought that was the last thing her ass needed right now. But, when in Rome...she made her way to the table and downed a round with them. It burned going down and by now they all had had too much to drink. She smiled and joined in on their conversation about the best make-up sex. Now that she had plenty of experience in.

Jordan had given up on trying to be a good boy. His bottle of pills was calling his name and so was Courtney. He grabbed his stash and his keys. He was feeling good and was sure that Courtney would have him feeling even better. He wouldn't have to go get it from anyone else if Jade had her ass home by now. He could feel his temper jabbing at him. Whenever he was feeling good it was like them damn cartoons with the devil and angel on his shoulders. The devil was getting the best of him. He might as well let Courtney ease his mind before he caught a case. He pulled up to the hotel. See that's what he was talking about. Courtney was classy. She always stayed in these nice ass hotels and he didn't even have to come out the pocket.

He clumsily texted her back that he was outside. She responded immediately, w*hy are you outside instead of up here inside of something else?* He smiled. Oh, yea Courtney was about to make his night, or morning, he glanced at the clock. Fuck Jade, he thought. Another text came through. Oh, now her ass wanted to be responding. He ignored her text and replied to Courtney. *On my way baby.* At the door, Courtney met him in a badass little number that showed more skin than it covered. She opened the door a little more and he saw that another girl was in the bed.

"We thought you weren't coming so we got started" Courtney tilted her head. "but of course, you're more than welcome to join us." He was undressing before the door closed. "This is Shay." Shay was hot. She was petite and part Asian. She was already naked and was lying in the bed pleasuring herself. "Or you can just watch." Courtney giggled. She crawled back in the bed with Shay. Jordan stood there for who knows how long watching them. Finally, he crawled in the bed between the two. "Ok, ok, I've seen enough. Let me get in on this action. I got something that's gonna turn this party up, he handed them both a pill."

Jade had gotten a message from Jordan saying that he was on his way up. His way up to where she wondered. She was about to ask him to pick her up. She had responded *Ok I'm at Leah's, come get me.* But, after several hours she'd given up and had decided to stay over to Leah's. She'd long left them downstairs partying feigning a headache. The more she thought about it the more she questioned Jordan's text. At about 530 am her phone went off with multiple texts back-to-back.

She thought, ok, he must have just realized she hadn't come home. She prepared herself for what she would find in the messages. She opened the messages sitting up. Her eyes adjusting to the dark photos that came across her phone. Several were of Jordan sprawled out on a bed naked. She squinted trying to make sure it was him. "What the fuck?" Several others followed of two women posing together. The last one was of the three of them. She threw her phone down. Trying not to hyperventilate, she picked up her phone again to look at the pictures as tears ran down her face. She tried looking for any clues of where he was, but she didn't have to look long.

The last message was an address and what she assumed was a room number. She opened her Uber app and scheduled a pick-up. She left the house quietly, not wanting to wake anyone. The girls were all sprawled out in the den.

No one had made it up to any of the bedrooms. She waited impatiently outside. Before she could convince herself otherwise, she had the driver drop her off at the hotel. She muttered, "oh had money to be up in one of the top hotels in the city huh."

She wished she had gone home before coming, so she wouldn't be empty-handed. It was probably for the best assault carried a different charge with a weapon. It was early morning and the sun had barely gotten up in the sky. It would have been a beautiful morning if she were here under different circumstances. She walked into the beautiful establishment and a nice young man greeted her at the front desk. "Good morning mam. Do you have a reservation?" "I sure as hell do." "Excuses me, mam?"

"No sir, I'm meeting a friend." She responded as she headed to the elevator. At the door, she hesitated. What exactly was she going to do when she got in there? She stood outside the door for a few minutes. She leaned up with her ear against the door, but the room was quiet.

She put her head down and turned away from the door. What was the use? It wouldn't be the first time she'd caught Jordan in bed with another woman. She'd even been arrested for attacking the female she'd caught him with. The only difference was that she had been in her own home. She'd probably make the news in this area because she was sure if she walked up in there now, she was capable of murder. She turned and left.

She drove around aimlessly for hours dreading heading home. The pictures and few minutes of sleep had sobered her. She was hurting. Seriously hurting. How many times did she have to keep going through this shit with him? She finally pulled into her driveway; Jordan's car was parked. She hurried up to the door ready for war. She stormed through the house slowly, thinking what if the pictures were old? But quickly dashed that idea, it came from his phone and it was him. Whether lately or old it had to occur while they were together and what were the odds that it wasn't last night? She could hear the shower running. Jordan was humming in the shower fueling her anger. She turned around and headed into the kitchen grabbing the largest knife in the block. She looked at her reflection in the knife, not recognizing her reflection. Without thinking she marched up to the door and kicked it opened. "You son of a bitch!" "What the fuck!" Jordan yelled scrambling out of the shower. He stood naked, water dripping from his body.

What woman could resist this man she asked herself. As he stood before her, she admired his body despite her anger. He was a god. Tatted and ripped. It took a moment for him to notice the knife. "Yo Jade baby what is wrong?" She walked up to him slowly holding the blade out. "I ought to cut your dick off since you like slinging it around everywhere." He stood still. "Jade don't fuck with me. Put that damn knife down."

She twirled the knife in her hand "Where exactly would you like me to put it at?" Her eyes wild. He tried getting her to look him in the eyes, but she wouldn't. "Where's Jordan?!" She fisted the handle holding the blade over her head. "Why wasn't I ever enough for you? Why do you have to keep putting me through this? I'm a good woman!" She shouted. I hate you she swung the blade blindly.

He jumped back, slipping on the wet floor before regaining his balance. She continued shouting I hate you!" She cut into the shower curtain behind him. "I hate you for what you have done to me. You took away everything from me. My sanity. Having me running around here all insecure and shit. I gained weight stressing over you. I left a good job. Stopped going to school! You took everything from me and gave me nothing in return." She threw the knife at him. It landed in the curtain before falling to the floor. "You gave me nothing but heartache and damn STD's from sleeping with any and everybody! If I thought I could survive in jail or deserved to be there I would have killed you in your sleep a long time ago." She turned away from him "I'm done. Done you hear me? As far as I'm concerned your dead to me." "Jade wait" he tried reaching for her. "Don't before I change my mind and do what I came in here to do." "Wait, Jade. Baby, please. I don't even know what I did wrong?" She shouted. "You don't know what you did wrong. Where the fuck was you last night!?"

He shouted back "Where the fuck was I? Where the fuck were you? I've been home. You the one just walking up in here! Coming in here all crazy and shit. You feeling guilty since your ass was out all night?"

"Don't you dare try to spin this on me! Why don't you check your phone? Does room 326 sound familiar to you?" He stammered then recovered. "I don't know what in the fuck you are talking about." "No? Let me refresh your memory." She pulled out her phone. "Dark hair, brown eyes. She's kind of cute if you like those porn chicks. Oh, and let's seen, Asian eyes, long black hair, perky breast that stand on their own." She shoved the phone in his face. "And your ass dead in the middle of them!"

He was speechless. "Oh, now you at a loss for words I see. Looks like ya'll had a real good time. So why don't you go on back over there? Matter fact. Pack all your shit before I burn it all down with your ass in the middle of it!" She knew that she was talking just to hear herself. She couldn't put him out. She had tried multiple times. He'd refuse to leave like he always did and wait for her because she always forgave him. She grabbed her keys and bag. Not this time, she would have to find a place to stay because there was no way in hell she was coming back there. One of them would end up in prison and one in a body bag. She left him standing in the same place and slammed the door. The house shook from the force.

Shit, he couldn't lie his way out of this one. How in the fuck did she get those pictures? It had to be Courtney or Shay because the photos were from the inside of the room. He was fucked. He made a call to the office saying he wasn't feeling well. He wasn't since he didn't get much sleep and his stomach was queasy. That could have been from his long night of drinks among other things, or his recent events. He'd never seen Jade this angry. He'd really fucked up this time.

He threw on some shorts and a t-shirt, grabbing a beer out of the refrigerator. He needed something stronger, but it was all he had. Besides, it would help ease his stomach and his mind.

Jade was on autopilot. She didn't know where she was going, she just drove. Thoughts of him in the hotel replaying in her head. She was such a fool. She questioned whether it was worth living anymore. No why should she contemplate

killing herself? He's the one that should die. She wished he would die. Jade cried until she didn't have any more tears to left. She didn't know how long she'd sat in the driveway. Someone tapped on the window, and she looked up into Trevor's eyes. "Jade?" She broke down again. "Open the door, Jade." She screamed and shouted. Trevor banged on the window. "Open the damn door Jade before I break the window!"

Trevor didn't know what was going on, but Jade looked like a madwoman. He thought about calling Leah but before he had a chance, she quit screaming and just stared at him. "Jade? Jade" he yelled. She wasn't moving. She was mumbling to herself. Her eyes empty and void. He broke the back window and climbed into the backseat. He touched her shoulder. "Jade, answer me." Relief flooded through him when she turned to him. He leaned across the seat unlocking the front door. He then ran over to the driver's side, still calling her name. She said his name, but her voice lacked any emotion. "Come on Jade. Talk to me."

Come inside. It's hot out here. He called his sister. "Lea somethings wrong with Jade. I don't know he shouted. She was in the yard when I came outside. She looks off. She isn't talking, just spaced out. I'm scared Lea. Somethings wrong" He ran into the bathroom and grabbed a washcloth soaking it with cool water. He ran back to her. "How do you mean not responding?!"

"I don't know! She's just staring off. She's not talking. She's not doing anything! She's soaked in sweat. She didn't have the car running or the air on. It's like 90 degrees outside!" "How does her skin feel Trevor. Is it hot?" He touched her neck and forehead. "Yes. Jade," he kept calling her name.

"Ok, Trev she may have overheated. You need to cool her off. But not too quick." "I already have a cool washcloth. I'm calling 911!" "Wait, no. If she's not having any trouble breathing and she's awake wait until I get there." He looked into her lifeless eyes. "Jade, come on Jade talk to me." She was sitting up on the edge of the bed. He reached for her hand rubbing at her wrist. "You're scaring us, Jade. Leah's on the phone. You have to tell me what's wrong." "Trevor?" she said weakly.

"Oh, Jade. He grabbed her and hugged her. "You scared the hell out of me." She leaned into him. "I can't keep doing this. Please help me." Leah was in the background talking. Leah's voice registered to him. "Hey, Leah. Yea. I think she's ok. Her coloring is coming back and she's talking." He was still holding her hand staring at her. No, you go ahead and get ready for work. I'll call you if I need you. He hung up looking at Jade. "What happened? Let me get you some water." He didn't like how her voice sounded. He filled a glass with tap water from the sink in the guest bathroom and returned holding it to her lips. "Drink." She followed his command. "Ok, how do you feel?" "I just want to be loved." "Trev," she looked up at him. "Is that too much to ask for? To be respected. To be met half the way." She shook her head. "What did I ever do to deserve any of this. I can't go back there."

"Did he…" "No" she responded quickly. "But even that would have been better than this. I can't cry anymore. I can't take this pain anymore. I just want it all to end. To go away. Please make it go away." She leaned on him laying her head on his shoulder. She didn't want to think. The photos kept flashing in her mind. Then their last fight. She was humiliated for allowing herself to keep going through this. She grabbed the sides of her head. My head hurts. "Make it all go away", she whispered. She wanted to hurt Jordan. Like he'd hurt her. She also wanted her thoughts to stop. She kissed Trevor.

He stiffened inhaling deeply, "Jade, no." She ignored him touching her tongue against his skin. "I need this. I need you. Please" tracing her fingers across his skin. "Make me forget it all for now. She climbed into his lap straddling him. She looked him in his eyes. He was trying to fight it, but she knew what desire looked like. She kissed him. He pulled away from her.

"We can't," he said. "I know that you want me. I've seen how you've watched me when you thought I wasn't looking. If Jordan hadn't come home the other night you wouldn't have stopped me. Tell me I'm wrong." She wrapped her arms around his neck moving against him. The friction of their clothing and his hardness against her turning her on more. "See I can feel that you want me. She kissed him again and he gave into her. For a few moments, he indulged her, deepening their kiss before stopping her.

"Shit Jade. Don't do this." "Tell me you don't want me." She kissed him again. I need you to want me. For someone to want me. Just me." She sighed standing. "What was I thinking. I'm tired of being desperate." He stood too. Unsure of what to do with his hands he sat down sitting on them. Shaking his head, no, as if that would convince him. "Jade, I don't know what happened, but I know that whatever it was had you not thinking clearly. I- I can't take advantage of you when you're like this." A single tear fell down her face.

There was going to be hell to pay if he gave in. "I'm sorry Jade. I'm sorry that he keeps hurting you. I'm sorry that you dated him instead of me. That you're his instead of mine." He wiped her tear following its trail across her lips. "This isn't what you want." She looked so broken. "I love you, Jade. I think I always have. You are everything that a man could ask for in a woman. But you're his woman., and no he doesn't deserve you. But don't ask me to cross that line. He's my best friend and you're worth more than this." She looked away, but not before he saw the humiliation in her eyes. He dropped his hands because he didn't trust himself to continue touching her. "To answer your questions you are beautiful, desirable, sexy, and not just physically. I find everything about you attractive. I miss my friend, before Jordan. I know she's in there. You don't have to ask any man if you're attractive. You always were and you will always be. But what men find more attractive than physical traits you already have… strength, independence, and confidence. If you don't like the way you are being treated then leave. You deserve better. If you are not satisfied with the way you look, change it." With that, he walked out of the room.

Trevor left before he did something he would regret. He went for a walk to clear his mind and sexual frustrations. It was becoming harder to fight off his attraction for her and her advances. He didn't know if he'd be able to if she came at him again. Part of him felt that he was betraying Jordan but lately he has been feeling like Jordan deserved whatever he had coming. He didn't feel bad for not being loyal to this Jordan. Jordan fought so hard to not be like his father. But that is exactly who he had become. All of this was triggering his memories of his parents. He was thankful for the isolation here. It was quiet. He looked down on the homes below. The mountains and the landscape had a calming effect on him.

Jordan pulled up to Trevor's house. His anger increasing when he saw Jade's car. He'd come to talk to his best friend, and she was here? He slammed his car door. He had a feeling that something was going on between the two. His instincts were never off. That's why she was acting differently. He walked around the house peering into the windows, holding his breath. He didn't know what he would do if he saw them together. His pity party was over after several drinks. He decided to take a drive and look for Jade, but she wasn't in any of her usual places. So, he decided to hit Trevor up and fill him on everything. He needed his advice. Things were still the same between them but now knew why. He walked back around to the front yelling out Jade's name.

Jade was in the guest room pacing. She couldn't believe she'd just embarrassed herself coming on to Trevor again. This time she didn't have the luxury of blaming it on the alcohol. Lately, her thoughts were all over the place. She'd been acting out of character. She was emotional. The more she tried to get things back to normal, the worst things became. She walked to the window when she heard someone yelling. She peered out the window but didn't see anyone. She heard someone call her name. Shit was that Jordan's voice. She heard him shout her name again. It was Jordan. She shook off her anxiety and went to the door. This was not going to go well. But he was the one wrong here. She tugged

on the anger she had for strength and opened the door.
"What do you want Jordan. I told you we were done. Now
you're following me?"

"You and Trevor. I knew something was up! I knew
you weren't shit!" If only he knew. Shrugging her shoulders,
she said, "So what if I am." She was playing a dangerous
game, but she wanted him to know how it felt. He moved so
quickly she didn't have time to shut the door. He shoved his
foot in the doorway "Where is he?" he shouted angrily.

He shoved her out of the way. "Yall got me fucked
up if you think I'm gonna let shit go down like this!" She
could smell the alcohol sweating from his pores. He stood in
the doorway his chest rising and falling. He went to the guest
room first, then upstairs to Trevor's room.

"This bitch thinks I'm playing with her. Here I am
feeling sorry for her ass and the whole time she is fucking my
boy!" "You're so fucking stupid," she muttered. I wish I
were fucking him." "What did you just say?" He turned to
her. "You know I've been letting your smart-ass mouth slide
lately. He walked up to her "so you want to fuck my boy."
She flinched as he raised his hand slapping the wall next to
her head. "I'm only going to ask you one more time what the

fuck are you doing here? You and Trev got something going on?"

"No Jordan." "Then why you seem to always be up in his face. Now you up in his house?!" She didn't have an answer for him. All the sass was gone. She'd only ever seen Jordan this upset once, and she never wanted to see him that way again. She tried to regain control by touching him on the shoulder. She had to get him out of here before Trevor came back. She saw him leave, but she didn't know how far he'd gone. He hadn't come back in, and she was sure that he could hear their raised voices. "I-I-I" she stammered. I came looking for Leah. That's all. She wasn't at home and checked by here. That's all I swear." She looked over her shoulder towards the door. "Although you treat me like shit. I've never played you Jordan. I've never so much as looked at another man and if I did it sure as hell wouldn't be Trevor."

Jordan backed up, distrust still in his eyes. "So where is he then? Let me see him and ask him myself." "I don't know. He let me in to wait for Leah and he left." "Why didn't you let me explain myself Jade?" he whined. "Those pics were from a long time ago. But you always jumping to conclusions." He rubbed his hand across his face. "At least let me explain. Talk to me baby." She swallowed "Ok".

"Ok? Ok, let's go for a ride." He walked towards to door. She followed.

She would play it cool to get him away from the house. That was better than him and Trevor hitting heads. She didn't want to come between them, and she was afraid of what would happen if Trevor came back. She was following Jordan to the car the same time Trevor walked up. "Jade? Are you alright?"

"You know I'm about sick of hearing you ask *my* girl if she's alright. What are you? Her fucking knight in shining armor? What I don't understand is why she seems to like running her ass over here to you?" "Well maybe if you were acting like a man she wouldn't have to. Instead of running around here acting like a little boy." Trevor stood his feet spread apart in a fighter stance. Jade reached out grabbing his hand. "It's ok Trevor. Really. I'm just going to go talk to Jordan. Let Leah know I'll be right back."

Leah? What was she talking about? Leah was at work. He raised a brow. She stood in front of Jordan blocking his view. She leaned in and kissed Jordan. "I'm ready baby. Come on" she said pulling his arm toward the car. But Jordan didn't move. She looked back at Trevor pleadingly.

"Whatever" Trevor said. He was tired of being sucked into their warped sense of love.

He walked into the house shutting the door. He watched from the window as Jade continued to plead with Jordan. It was something about the way she was standing that made him watch closer. He saw that she was trembling. She kissed Jordan again saying something to him. He got into the car and she ran to the passenger side. He sped off tires squealing.

"So, you gonna keep this bullshit up trying to play me? What the fuck are we doing over to Trev's Jade?" "I told you Jordan I was waiting for Leah. That's all." She was getting tired of his whirlwind of emotions and bull. "Besides, you have a lot of nerve huffing and puffing around here after last night." She hit the dash "And don't feed me that bullshit about those pics being old. You forgot you sent me a picture last night?"

He turned to her. "I was not there last night. You'd know that if you were home." She folded her hands across her chest. "Whatever Jordan. If all you came to do was lie to me you could have left me where I was, and slow down." "Picture that. Me leaving you over to Trevor's house. Yall niggas got me fucked up. So, you want Trevor huh? You always did have a thing for them rugged ass niggas. Don't let his good boy bull shit fool you. He ain't shit either. How long ya'll two been hooking up? You think I'm really about to let you leave me for my boy?" His eyes were wild, as he picked up more speed.

She sat up "Jordan slow down. Why don't you pull over and let me drive?" "Don't change the subject Jade! He shouted rubbing his nose. "You must have a death wish. Fucking my best friend!" "I am not sleeping with him Jordan! What do you want from me?"

"The truth for starters. It's all good. Cats out the bag now. You might as well fess up." "She threw her hands up. Whatever Jordan. Think whatever you want! Take me back. This conversation is over!" "Oh no we are just getting started." He reached over shoving her head into the window. "Since you want to act like a hoe, let me show you how I treat hoes." She held her head where she'd hit it against the window.

"Jordan! You said you wouldn't hit me again! She reached across the seat slapping him. He laughed rubbing at his nose before grabbing by the throat. "You are not leaving me you stupid bitch!" He shouted. She pulled at his fingers trying to pry them from around her throat. "You are mine, remember that" before shoving her away! She gasped for air. "You son of a bitch! I hate you! I hate you! I do not love you! Who could love you! You are hateful, deceitful. A liar and a woman beater. You let me out of this car now or I'm calling the police." She reached for her phone.

Jordan continued driving, picking up more speed. She glanced at the speedometer. He was doing close to 90 miles an hour. She dialed Trevor's number. She wasn't sure why and not 911. When he answered she told him "He's gonna kill us."

"Who are you talking to?" He reached for her phone and she pulled away from him. He slapped her and grabbed the phone putting it on speaker. "You called him? Tell me, Trevor, tell me you fucking Jade?" "What Jordan hell no. Where are ya'll at? Don't do anything stupid Jordan. Nothing is going on between Jade and me. Come back to the house and talk to me man to man."

"Naw I'm good. Since she likes calling on you so much, let's see if she'll be calling out for you when I kill her ass." He slowed as they came to a curve, but at the last second, he let off the brakes looking at her. "Are you willing to die for that nigga? Thought you were gonna leave me for that nigga." He swerved hitting a tree, never taking his eyes off her as they made impact. Trevor's name was the last thing she called out.

Trevor was shouting both of their names. He ran to his car. Jade shouted out before the impact Willow's Peak. He drove in that direction. Damn, they had made it far in the short time since Jordan left the house. He hadn't prayed in a long time, but he prayed all the way there. He heard the sirens before reaching them. Blue and red lights were off in the distance. The road was already blocked off. He could see someone performing CPR on the ground. He yelled out Jade's name. An officer stopped him. Do you know who was in this vehicle? Yes, my best friend Jordan and his wife Jade. He tried getting past the officer, but he held him back. He could make out Jade on the ground as they lifted her onto a gurney running towards the ambulance. He looked around for Jordan. He looked to the officer "Jordan?" Where's my friend Jordan?" "We only found the girl. A civilian was working on her when we arrived." At that moment he heard shouting from the woods.

"We have another one someone shouted". He knew before they brought him out that Jordan was gone. There was no way he would have survived being thrown that far out. He didn't want to see him. "Which hospital did they take her to?"

"Mercer is the nearest trauma center." He heard the other officers talking he faintly heard male, intoxicated as he ran to his car. His heart racing. Damn Jordan why man? He prayed more as he drove to the hospital. He couldn't bring himself to call Leah or anyone until he knew for sure.

He arrived at the hospital and asked for Jade Rivers. "Are you a family member?" He called Leah, then. "Leah it's Jordan and Jade. They were in an accident, and I think Jordan's…" he couldn't bring himself to say it. There was no way his friend was gone. Instead, he said. "Jade was rushed to your hospital. It's serious Leah. They aren't telling me anything because I am not family. Jade. She has no family Leah. Please check on her. Please."

It was hours before they allowed them to see Jade. He sat there until Leah came and told him that she was out of surgery. Thankfully, Jade had made Leah power of attorney. It was Leah's idea. He was Leah's and Jordan's. All their parents were gone. Leah leads him down the hall as she tried preparing him for what he'd see.

The bed and equipment seemed to swallow her up. Tubes were everywhere and the machines beeped and whirred. Her chest rose and fell with the sound of the machine that was breathing for her. Nothing could prepare

him for what he saw. He touched her hand, and it was cold.
He placed the blanket across her fingers. "She can hear us
Jordan, I know she can."

"Jade, he whispered. He leaned over as close as he
could and spoke in low tones to her. I'm so sorry Jade. I'm
sorry I let you leave with him. I'm sorry this happened. Please
fight baby girl. Hang on." He looked back at Leah who was
fighting back tears. He walked back towards her and hugged
her. "She's going to be ok Trev. She has to."

Jade opened her eyes slowly. It was so cold. She
couldn't move her head. She focused on a nurse who was
calling her name. "Hi, Jade. Take it easy. You are in the
hospital. You were in an accident." Her body felt so heavy.
She moaned. "Jordan?"

The nurse looked away before saying "Jordan's not
here. We need to know how you feel Jade. You have been in
a coma for over a month. Do you remember what
happened?" She shook her head and the room rotated. "I was
with Jordan." She tried sitting up but couldn't. "Why is this
blanket so heavy? The nurse looked concerned. "Let me get
the doctor."

"Wait. Can you call my friend Trevor?" "He's here.
He ran down for coffee, I believe." The doctor appeared

before her, shining a light into her eyes. "Jade, can you tell me where you are?" "In the hospital, is what the nurse told me." "And do you remember what happened?" "I was in an accident. We were in an accident. My husband and I." "Do you know what year it is?" "Two thousand nineteen" "Ok, good. Can you squeeze my fingers?" she did but it was draining."

"I'm so tired and why does it feel like something is on top of my legs?" She picked up the concern in his eyes. "Jade tell me do you feel this?" "Feel what?" She waited but didn't feel anything. "What am I supposed to be feeling? I'm so tired. She closed her eyes welcoming the familiar darkness.

Stay tuned for "Fit to Love..."

CPSIA information can be obtained
at www.ICGtesting.com
Printed in the USA
LVHW031319211221
706818LV00001B/150